To cheque

R. Kinba

TWO MINUTES TO LIVE—
TEN SECONDS TO DIE

TWO MINUTES TO LIVE— TEN SECONDS TO DIE

The Conflicts of Police Officers and Politics

BILL KINKADE

iUniverse, Inc.
Bloomington

Two Minutes To Live—Ten Seconds To Die
The Conflicts of Police Officers and Politics

iUniverse books may be ordered through booksellers or by contacting:

iUniverse
1663 Liberty Drive
Bloomington, IN 47403
www.iuniverse.com
1-800-Authors (1-800-288-4677)

ISBN: 978-1-4759-0094-1 (sc)
ISBN: 978-1-4759-0095-8 (ebk)

Printed in the United States of America

iUniverse rev. date: 03/08/2012

CHAPTER 1

IT WAS GOING ON FOUR o'clock in afternoon and in late March the Texas sun wouldn't hang in the sky near as late is it would in just a few weeks. Then, daylight savings time would coincide with the further tilt of the earth to produce the long, hot days of summer in south Texas. For now, the sun was at just the right position in the bright blue sky to create a perfect canvass for the Fort Worth skyline.

Toby had the Camaro on a comfortable cruising speed of 60mph but as his eyes shifted right, he noticed the clock and was reminded that he had to be at roll-call at 6:00pm. He stepped on the gas pedal and the powerful engine jumped quickly to 70mph. He wanted to have enough time to eat dinner and visit with his mom and dad, but he was always apprehensive about being late for roll-call.

He held his speed steady as he pushed the button on his *Bluetooth* ear-piece and told the computer voice to "Dial Mom and Dad-home."

His dad answered at the start of the second ring. "Dad, this is Toby, I'm on my way. I just turned north onto I-820, so I'm about fifteen minutes out. Tell Mom to get the roast out of the pot. I want to have plenty of time to visit while we eat and you know how I am about roll-call. Yeah, I'll have a couple of new stories but nothing too exciting. I don't want to get Mom's worry-meter going any more than normal; she's got enough to deal with. Ok, see you in a few. Bye."

The Camaro was purring along nicely and he let his thoughts slide back over the sequence of events that led him to where he was today; Patrolman, Toby Roberts of the Plainfield, Texas Police Department.

Toby was physically fit by anyone's definition. He was an even 6'tall and held his weight at 185lbs; the weight was mostly muscle and combined with his close cut, sandy brown hair and pale blue eyes his appearance belied his weight and strength. In high school, he had tried out for soccer and by the end of his freshman year, he was already a star of the team and the subject of conversations among parents, coaches, and fans of soccer in the Dallas-Ft Worth area.

By his junior year, he was in the newspapers every Monday morning as the top scorer or best defensive playmaker in the weekend games between the area schools. Then in his senior year, he was selected to play on a team consisting of the elite high school players from all of the DFW area in a league that included similar teams from all over Texas, and conferences encompassing the Eastern half of the United States. The league was separate from the high school conferences, and was scouted regularly by the top colleges and occasionally the pros.

Upon graduation, Toby was the guest at three or four prestigious universities and received offers of full-ride scholarships from all of them. It was a whirlwind of excitement, and the promise of an exciting four years of college and then on into the pros. Everyone assured him he had the talent to make it all the way. His dad was his biggest fan and supporter.

Darren Roberts' job required him to travel all over the country for a large developer of shopping centers. He took his job seriously, but he never doubted his most serious job was the happiness and well being of his wife and three sons. All four were totally aware of the commitment he had made to that mission in his life.

While everyone in the family was caught up in the excitement about—what looked like—the future for Toby Roberts, a total shift in paradigm was taking place in Toby. It was difficult to explain, even to understand, but one day it hit him. Playing soccer was fun and it had taught him important truths about his own abilities but more importantly, the value of teamwork while trying to move the ball to the goal. He had the good judgment and the unique ability to render sound decisions in the face of immediate peril and claim victory from the jaws of impending defeat. The thought that kept pestering his practical thinking process was: then what?

He had come to the dinner table one evening and announced—to everyone's astonishment—that he didn't think he wanted to play soccer any longer. He was thinking about turning down all the scholarships and going to the local college that offered a degree in Criminal Investigation. He said his goal was to become a police officer. His family was momentarily stunned.

Darren Roberts looked across the dining table and asked, "Toby, you have proven to everyone that you have very special talents on the soccer field. What makes you think you want to be a policeman? I've never heard you talk about that idea before?"

"Dad, I know this is a shock to you—to all of you, and I admit it is something I'm still getting used to. I have given it a lot of thought, and I feel right down in my heart and soul, that the skills I've developed in soccer will serve me well in most aspects of police work. I would as a policeman, be serving my community in a way that would make me feel proud, every day, to get up and go to work; just like you do, when you build a big shopping mall that gives the people a better place to shop and makes your company a profit at the same time. Do you understand that?"

His dad had sat still for what seemed like the longest time, looking straight into his eyes. Then he spoke.

"Toby, as long as you believe what you just said, I'll support you one hundred percent, and I predict you will make one of the best damned police officers in the State of Texas."

His mother, harboring an instinctive feeling of apprehension, had reluctantly agreed and with a loving smile on her face and a look of knowing admiration in her eyes, said, "If you're finished, Toby, go out in the kitchen and bring the apple pie sitting on the stove."

That had pretty much ended soccer as the dominate subject of dinner-table conversation although it remained a backup subject when a spectacular play, high school, college, or professional made the news.

Toby brought himself back to his driving, changed lanes and exited I-820 and began winding into the sprinkling of newer homes. His dad had purchased this house just two years ago and even though it was just he and Mom now, they had selected the home for its desirable location. It was close to his older brother and their two adorable kids; a boy, now four, and his two year old sister. Grandpa and grandma did all they could to spoil the kids rotten. Toby's older brother, Scott, and his wife, Marcie, were guilty accomplices.

Scott had opened his own computer software company and in the first year produced a management-control program for oil exploration companies, and within two more years, had a string of successful programs that brought big money in every year; his company was getting bigger by the day. The kids had everything they wished for and more.

He slowed the Camaro as he turned into the driveway. The two-story house, on a one acre lot, sat back from the street about 100' and the wide driveway led him up to the three-car garage.

The pork roast and all the trimmings were on the table and as soon as the hugs were over, they all sat down. Dad said grace and the conversation moved from Dad's newest project in California to questions about Toby's recent patrols and what exciting encounters he had experienced.

Toby had graduated from the local college with a respectable set of grades and a number of special mentions and certificates of achievement from professors and visiting law enforcement teachers on his diligence in thinking through legal questions that required thorough research and thought.

Never the less, when he finished college, the economy had done a lot of damage to the cities and county budgets throughout the Metroplex. There were no openings in the Dallas-Ft. Worth area for a rookie cop.

He had spent the next 18 months flipping burgers for *McDonalds*, and cashiering at *Starbucks*; boring, but instructive in developing patience. Starbucks helped him with communication skills and customer service. Toby soaked it all up but yearned for the blue uniform, service revolver, and his own patrol.

The break came from an unexpected source. Toby had thought the sheriff's department, in either of the two large counties, would offer the best chance of an opening, if for no other reason than size.

The city of Plainfield had a reputation in the DFW area of professional excellence in its police department. Toby had applied, thinking that if he got on there, he would get the most thorough training on techniques and procedures—than any of the other municipalities or counties. When the city of Plainfield called and said they had an opening and wanted him in for an interview, he couldn't take off his Starbucks apron fast enough.

Plainfield was a major, growing community in the DFW Metroplex. It was initially developed as a residential community for people who weren't comfortable with the multi-cultural nature of the growing cities of Dallas, Ft. Worth and other suburbs; but wanted to stay in the midst of the dynamic growth that was bringing wealth and prosperity to the area.

One Sunday afternoon, a group that was discussing the options that seemed viable, gathered at the home of one of the members. After a refill of the wine glasses the host brought out a map of the area, showing each municipality in the metro-plex. He brought everyone's attention to an area—smack in the middle—that had not been included in any of the previous incorporated cities.

The State of Texas had reserved the choice acreage for a branch campus for research and development for The University of Texas. The man was an alumni and had confidential information the hold on the location was about to be released. If the group made the right connections now and the right contribution to the football program at the University, the man felt sure they would allow the group to put a claim on it for their new city. A city they could build from the ground-up to meet their own *standards*.

Now, fifteen years later, their growth was exceeding their wildest imaginings in unforeseen ways. Wealth and influence, which they welcomed, were accompanied by an unexpected mix of lower economic and social groups. Blue collar workers that found jobs in Plainfield figured out ways to live there; criminal elements found business opportunities there. A bigger police force that they had planned for was required. Their standards required their police department be the best and reflect the character of the city fathers.

None of this was known to Toby nor would it have deterred him from the appointment—even if he had known all the secret motivations of every official in Plainfield. In Toby's thinking, that was politics and he was not interested in politics. He just wanted to get on the job, use the knowledge he had picked up in school, add the training that a good department would provide, and finish off with some on-the-street experience.

He had shown up for the interview; early by fifteen minutes. He was nervous, but tempered with confidence. He knew this was where he was supposed to be and the job was what he was meant to be doing.

There were two other applicants, both younger than him; one just out of school and the other one was just two weeks out of the army with one year as an MP in Iraq. They might be competition. The interviews were long and seemed tedious. He left with no clear feeling of how the interviewing officer might be leaning, however, he thought he did great! A week later, he got the letter in the mail. The interview process was complete and he was to report to the academy the following Monday to begin training.

The routine at the academy was tough but Toby loved the challenge and excelled at every level. He received certificates of excellence in all categories and at each level. He led the class in the physical training sessions; quick and agile, and he could run the five miles with a thirty pound pack and finish by himself with time for a coffee before the next runner arrived. The whole family came for his graduation. It was a special event in the life of Toby Roberts.

The graduating class was only eight in number. Six men and two women were about to be added to the ranks. It had become the policy for Plainfield PD to deliberately add women and minorities to the rank and file. This policy was not to reflect the population of Plainfield as much as to comply with regulations of the Federal Government; from whom a chunk of the money was coming to pay the salaries of the additions.

CHAPTER 2

Aﬀer a two week assignment in headquarters, honing his ability to please the paper pushers, Toby was finally assigned to a training officer to begin patrols. The short stint in headquarters exposed him to an atmosphere very new and different than that at the academy. The academy had been all about PROTECT and SERVE the citizens of Plainfield but at headquarters—it was more image and political correctness; Toby shrugged-it-off as not something for a policeman on patrol to worry about.

Most of Plainfield was middle and upper class residential areas with the usual neighborhood characteristics. It had a pretty good sized shopping mall at the intersection of two interstates, a downtown made up mostly of banks, city hall, municipal courts and enough office buildings for the lawyers, insurance agents, accountants and influence-peddlers that made their living from the activities of the rest.

The mayor, and a majority of the city council, was made up of people who had already made their wealth from—at least in part—decisions made and policies set by previous councils or themselves since taking office. These directions and/or rules were always couched in words and publicly discussed in a manner that massaged the citizenry's desire for a public image of being sensitive to the little people, the downtrodden, etc. True enough, there weren't hardly any of those kind of citizens in Plainfield but just the thought kept most of the residents walking around with heads held high, and sleeping sound with their consciences clear.

Toby's thoughts returned to dinner with his folks as he grabbed a couple of bowls from the counter and carried them into the dining room.

"Toby, be careful and don't spill anything on that beautiful blue uniform," his mom cautioned.

"You can rest assured of that. Don't worry, Mom, I'm very careful to avoid giving the sergeant any reason to chew my ass out for food stains on the uniform. He finds enough other crap to give me a bad time about."

Darrin Roberts came into the dining room, in time to hear Toby's last remark and with a look of concern, asked, "What did you do to get on the sergeant's bad side, Toby?"

"It's not personal Dad. His job is to finish the process of making me the best cop in the City of Plainfield."

Dinner was great and the family got in all their questions and comments. Everybody told him how proud they were and Mom gave him a rib-breaking hug and told him to be careful and to plan on giving another report over another dinner in about a week.

After dinner, they all said good-bys and Toby paused at the mirror and adjusted his hat until it was just right, then went out to the Camaro and headed it back to Plainfield.

CHAPTER 3

A T 6:00PM, THE SHIFT SERGEANT entered the room and yelled for everyone to sit down and listen up. He read off the patrol assignments and then picked up his clipboard and began up-dating the precinct on wants, APBs, and any criminal activities that might affect their patrols.

Plainfield did not have a crime problem like other cities with a population of 500,000. But, consistent with the rest of America, they did have one: Drugs. The pushers in Plainfield were confident that their customers would always be able to pay for their purchases. Most of the drugs that came into Plainfield were funneled through a system tightly controlled in supply and distribution. Occasionally, there was a maverick that needed to raise his working capital and would use burglary or robbery to obtain free merchandise and the funds to buy back into the supply chain. The organized part of the trade tried to discourage that kind of free enterprise ingenuity but was not totally successful.

The sergeant wrapped up the roll-call and the 6:00pm-2:00am shift, headed for the cars.

Toby and partner Sonny Montgomery began their patrol in the normal pattern. They took a close look at the "hangers" at the 7-Eleven's and checked two businesses who had reported unexplained pry-marks around their back doors. Some underfunded addict was trying to get back in the supply chain.

At 11:00pm they stopped at their favorite all-night coffee shop. Toby was trying to guard the waist-line, so he passed on the butter-horn and just sipped his coffee. Sonny, who seemed to burn calories just sitting in the patrol car, had an extra large pastry, heated, with a big pad of butter. He finished the delicacy before Toby finished his coffee.

Back in the car, Sonny asked how Toby's younger brother was doing. Todd Roberts had been the problem child for his parents. He was four years younger than Toby and in the pre-teen years, he seemed to follow in his brothers footsteps. He had skills on the soccer field that led coaches, parents, and players to talk about the Robert's dynasty that seemed to be in-the-making. Then Todd took a sudden turn to trouble. He experimented with marijuana like most of his age group. He migrated, quickly, to the harder and more powerful drugs and it wasn't long before his behavior attracted the attention of his soccer coach, teachers, and ultimately the police. The next few years were a nightmare of events; expulsion from school, cut from the soccer team, numerous arrests and appearances in front of a judge who started out sympathetic but was eventually angry at Todd's apparent lack of respect for the law and the police and the courts responsible for enforcement of the laws; Todd seemed to have contempt for them all.

"Todd's coming along. He got a job three months ago at Big Idea Burgers and so far, has not failed to show up for work one time. He has not missed a meeting with his PO in that same time frame and he has a girl friend that he is living with. She is going to the community college and working part time as a waitress. He comes over about once a week and eats dinner with the folks, which makes them happy."

Sonny said, as he watched the street, "Your folks have been real troopers with that boy."

"No, they've just been parents, as they define parenthood. They wouldn't be any different with any of us boys," Toby insisted.

CHAPTER 4

O N THE NORTH-EAST CORNER OF the patrol area that Toby and Sonny were assigned to on this night, Tarrant Street was only two blocks long. The entire two blocks consisted of small retail shops on the north side and small professional offices on the south. The shops were a mix of neighborhood convenience stores; beauty nails, tanning, and—in the middle of them all—was Harold's Drug Store, one of the few surviving independent drug stores and pharmacies. The offices across the street were doctors of different specialties, a lawyer, insurance agent, etc.

The buildings were connected together in a row with only the cross street of Sixth Avenue, separating each row of shops from its duplicate in the next block. There was on-street parking in front and a wide alley that ran the full two blocks distance in the rear.

The alley was large enough to accommodate the large garbage dumpsters and leave enough room for two employee cars, so they would not take spaces on the street.

Donald "Bones" Lindsay drove the large model Pontiac, slowly, along Tarrant Street looking at both sides of the street as he passed the darkened store-fronts, almost stopping in front of Harold's Drug's. He wanted to make sure no one was taking a late night stroll or some drunk was just feeling his way home from the neighborhood tavern ten blocks to the south. He also needed to make sure Harold was not working late tonight. It was one o'clock in the morning and he figured all the activity in this neighborhood was done for the night. He wanted to wait until later but he couldn't. His hands were starting to shake worse than normal and he was afraid that another hour of denying himself the oxycodone he needed, and he might not be able to perform the necessary task to do the job.

"Bones" got his nickname from his physical build. He had always been thin but since he had started on the pain killers, his weight had dropped off further; his appetite, for anything but the drug, seemed to follow the weight loss.

He had planned this job carefully. One of the store clerks, for fifty bucks and the promise of some pain pills, had given him the code to the alarm at the pharmacy. While appearing to be a customer, he had observed the pharmacist unlocking the wood cabinet where he kept the controlled stuff. The idiot; it surly didn't meet the government's rules for that type of storage. Oh well, it would make his job that much easier tonight.

He turned the Pontiac onto Sixth Avenue, shut off the lights, and turned into the alley. He liked the car. He had watched the owner drive it home and park it on the street in front of the apartment building just as he did on other nights when he retired for the evening. It only took a couple of minutes to connect the right wires and drive away. He stopped the Pontiac with the passenger doors right by the back door to the pharmacy. He left the motor running. It would be too much trouble to restart, if he needed to do a fast get away. He retrieved a short handled pry-bar from the back floor of the Pontiac. His plan was to pop the door and go quickly to the alarm panel and input the code. That would turn off the alarm and give him plenty of time to open the cabinet and bag the contents. It was going to be a sweet job. He began to apply the bar to the back door.

Bones was not a novice at burglary. It had become an essential practice in financing his addiction to the various drugs, which now seemed to make daily demands on his body. He'd gotten his introduction to drugs, like so many youths in America, in junior high school. At first, it was simple curiosity. Trying something he'd never done before. Being dared to try smoking a joint, carried a sense of bravery and declining the challenge made any kid feel cowardly and disgraced in front of their peers.

Immediately, money became a problem. There weren't any more free samples. He could have stopped then, but he liked the feeling of being high. He hadn't had many opportunities to do something—just because it made him feel good, in the few years that had been his life, so far.

Lindsay's folks were working, poor people. His dad was a night watchman at a warehouse in the industrial district and his mom cleaned houses for "Molly Maids," a franchise that paid minimum wage. There was barely enough for bare necessities; never, any money for Bones to do something, just to feel good.

He discovered, quickly, that he was good at stealing things and not getting caught. He volunteered to go with his mother, though it was against company rules, and while she was busily cleaning, he would take small jewelry items that wouldn't be missed right away and might later be thought of as misplaced or lost. Shoplifting was easy because he felt no guilt and was never suspected by store clerks. Most of the kids got caught, he figured, because their guilty conscience showed like a neon sign, all over their faces.

Not Bones, no sir. He didn't give a shit. The store had more than they could sell anyway, and he deserved to have his share. He could pocket $50-$100 worth of stuff in his baggy pants pocket and walk right by the sales clerk and shrug his shoulders with a look of disappointment on his face and say, "Well I hope you get some more in next week."

The sales clerks never bothered him. He figured it was mostly because they didn't give a shit, either. In fact, he thought they were probably carrying their share home every week, just like him.

He graduated briefly to cocaine but it was too expensive for the lift he got from it. He got his first shot of Tar Heroin while he was in high school and soon decided he would skip school and concentrate on things that made him feel good, or nothing at all.

He had been a courier, a street vendor, and when he was flush enough, a broker-middle man. The problem for Bones was, he always wound up broke and needing a fix real bad. He lived on the street. Sometimes sleeping at a cardboard hotel, Salvation Army Shelter, and from time to time, he would pop for a cheap motel room. Stealing remained the most reliable source of money for drugs.

Two years ago, when he was hurting real bad, a "meth cooker" offered him a needle as a sample. WOW! It was a total release and took him to places he'd never been; just numbness with all the crap in his life shut off. He'd heard about, and had seen first hand, some of the after effects and even though it scared him a little, logical thought escaped him when he needed the release from the pressure.

Prescription pills soon became part of his diet, and drug store burglary a new job skill.

He realized his hands were shaking, hard. He needed to get out of here. He'd been in the store too long. He needed to swallow some of the pills, but he had to get away from where he was. He knew the longer he stayed in a store, the more likely he might get caught. He began to hurry. He felt a panic.

CHAPTER 5

T OBY AND SONNY WERE CRUISING through the parking lot of the mall when they got the call.

"Car 1201, this is dispatch, we have a code 1011 in progress at 607 Tarrant, silent alarm. Acknowledge."

"Dispatch, this is car 1201, we are 10-20 at Prairie Mall, responding to silent alarm at 607 Tarrant. Estimate arrival in seven minutes. Over"

Toby ran with lights and siren most of the distance, then shut off siren and all lights as they cruised down Tarrant passed the pharmacy. The store was totally dark in front, which was a problem because the store was supposed to have a security light burning 24 hours a day. They went past the doors in the 600 block and turned at 7th Avenue, toward the alley. Toby moved the cruiser slowly into the alley and saw the silhouette of a car parked next to the back door, which was opened a crack. The car was facing toward Toby's cruiser and he could see by the back-light from the mercury-vapor light on a pole at 6th avenue, that it was emitting a vapor-laden exhaust.

"Dispatch, this is car 1201. We are 10-20 at the rear of Harold's Drugs, 607 Tarrant. Security light is not lit in the front area, back door is open and a small light is burning in the rear. We can see movement inside, and a car, with no lights burning, is parked by the back door and the motor is running. We request a back-up unit. 10-4?"

"Car 1201, this is dispatch, car 1216 is backing you; ETA four minutes."

Toby and Sonny waited about two minutes, and then saw the figure of a man come out of the back of the drug store. They heard the sound of the car door slamming.

"I think he just put the loot in the back seat and looks like he just closed the back door of the drug store," Sonny whispered.

"Yeah, he's coming around the back of the car. I can't see him good; the driver's door is open. I think we better light him up before he gets in the car," Toby said and engaged the radio.

"Dispatch, this is car 1201. Advise backup, we cannot wait. We're lighting up and initiating arrest."

Toby hit the light switch as he opened his door, P.A. microphone in hand.

"This is the police, stop what you're doing and put your hands on top of the car!"

The figure moved quickly, diving into the car. Toby stepped to his left, as Sonny took the right side of the alley and moved down toward the car. He heard the tires squeal as the motor roared and the car surged forward. He tried to go back to his right, to let the car pass between him and the back wall of the building, but the car kept turning toward him. Toby stepped again to the right, and at the last second, he twisted his body to the right, feeling the fender push against his thigh, butt, and hip. Before he could feel good about dodging the direct hit from the car, the driver's door; still partially opened, caught him on the left shoulder and spun him back to the left. He stumbled, but stayed on his feet.

Toby had pulled his Glock from its holster as he stood from the squad car—it was still in his hand, after the impact from the Pontiac. He had, apparently, yelled out when he was struck by the door and Sonny, and fearing his partner was injured, he started running back toward Toby. Somehow, amazingly, Toby was still on his feet and in possession of his firearm, which he raised and pointed at the passing and fleeing car. Ten shots with armor-piercing bullets from the 9mm Glock followed and struck the heavy car, which swerved to the right, striking one of the large garbage dumpsters, bouncing off and continuing erratically down the alley. Sonny then reached Toby's position and fired two more shots into the fleeing car. It twisted down the alley, crossed 6th avenue and crashed into a brick building across the street.

The building did not move!

Sonny turned and yelled, "Toby, are you OK?"

"I think so, check the guy in the car."

Sonny ran down the alley, gun drawn, and approached the wrecked car. The driver was hunched over the steering wheel, making sounds that were a mixture of cursing the pain and anger at the police. Blood was running from a cut on his forehead and a swelling was forming between his eyes from striking the steering wheel. A dark red stain was forming on the knit shirt around his left shoulder. He ordered the driver to exit the car. The man was screaming with pain, as Sonny fumbled with the door handle, but it was jammed. Sonny tried and concluded that it would have to be pried open, so he handcuffed the driver to the steering wheel.

Car 1216 squealed into the alley, lights flashing. Toby told the two officers he was okay but to call in "shots fired" to dispatch, then moved back over to his cruiser and sat down behind the steering wheel to let his head clear. He heard sirens in the distance and soon the scene was cluttered with police cruisers, ambulances, and uniforms. A CSI unit began working the pharmacy, the alley, and the crash site. The team from the Fire Department popped the door on the Pontiac and the EMTs determined that "Bones" had caught one round in his upper left arm, just below the shoulder and one in his left hip. Neither wound appeared to be life threatening but this guy was not going to enter any marathons or kick boxing matches for a long time.

The back-up team of cops, were veterans and some were quick to volunteer compliments and "well-done" to Toby and Sonny, but one of the officers cautioned Toby, "Just be careful what you say, who you say it to, and don't go into too much detail voluntarily; just wait for the questions."

Back at the 3rd precincts headquarters, Toby was told to go into one of the interview rooms with a legal pad and write, in his own words, everything he remembered about the incident. He thought about the words of caution from the officer at the crime scene but shrugged it off as rank and file paranoia with the command structure.

The process of recounting the events of the evening took longer than he thought it would. He finally finished his report. The sergeant took his gun and tagged it for ballistics, and advised Toby that he would be on administrative leave for three days. It was now 5:00am, Tuesday morning. He was to go home and try to get some sleep. On Wednesday, he was to report to the office of counseling and guidance for further review.

CHAPTER 6

TOBY CALLED HIS MOM AND dad on the way home and assured them he was ok and they should not be alarmed when the story hit the morning news. He then called his girlfriend, Karen, and assured her that nothing was wrong with him that five or six hours of sleep wouldn't cure and he was going to deal with that as soon as he got home. She said she would come by about five o'clock, before going to work and fix him something to eat.

The first thing Toby did when he arrived home was turn his phone off. Then, he undressed and set the shower as hot as his skin could tolerate and stepped in. He let the water beat on him until he felt the tension drain out of his body. He crawled into his bed and was instantly asleep. *It wasn't as peaceful as he normally slept; there were flashes of speeding cars, squealing tires, punctuated by the sound of gunfire. Once or maybe twice, he was aware of partial wakening, then a return to deep, peaceful, energy gaining sleep.*

Then, the sound of a drill motor—shrill and deadly; the over-sized bit was pointed right at the bridge of his nose. He was paralyzed with fear, unable to move. Nobody was holding him down but he seemed to be paralyzed, unable to move or cry out. He woke, sitting straight up in bed, and realized it was the front door bell, making its damnable, buzzing noise. He swung off the bed and pulled on a pair of jeans and a t-shirt. He opened the door, let Karen look him over good before they moved together in an embrace that needed no words; none were spoken for what seemed a very long time. He led Karen into the kitchen. She started a pot of coffee and poured orange juice.

He put his arms around her and pulled her close to him and just knowing that she was concerned, restored his confidence and general sense of well being.

Karen fixed Jimmy Dean Sausage, scrambled eggs, and a can of Pillsbury biscuits. After he consumed the meal, he told Karen the story and answered her questions. He told her to go on to work and he would see her tomorrow after he finished with the shrink.

"Toby is there a doctor who's supposed to help you with any guilt feelings or fears that might result from the shooting that would be a problem for you in future situations."

"I don't know, Karen. First of all, I don't have any guilt feelings. It was a clean shooting as far as I'm concerned. The guy tried to kill me. He used a car instead of a gun but in either case, if he'd succeeded, I'd be just as dead as if he'd shot me." Toby continued. "The counseling session is standard procedure when there's a shooting. Don't worry about it, in a few days, it will all blow over. Now you better get to work before they fire you."

She kissed him and reminded him to get some more sleep and be sharp for the counselor tomorrow.

CHAPTER 7

AFTER KAREN LEFT FOR WORK, Toby turned the phone on and made some obligatory calls. He assured Scott and Marcie he was okay and talked to both kids, reassuring them that Uncle Toby still loved them and would come see them real soon. It took much longer to address all the questions and relieve their concerns of Mom and Dad. Then it took more time to let them express their pride over what a fine police officer their son was.

After the calls, Toby got into the Camaro and drove toward the down town area. He soon realized he was close to The Precinct, a cop lounge and restaurant. He pulled into the parking lot and went inside. It was Tuesday night and business was naturally a little slow, but there were always customers at a cop bar.

Toby was not a drinker, but he had visited The Precinct before on the occasion of someone's birthday, promotion, or anniversary and had a beer. Four uniforms sat at a table off to his left, two he had met before and they called him over and stood and began congratulations. He joined them and ordered a Lone Star Beer in a long neck bottle.

He didn't stay long but as he walked out and slid into the Camaro, he felt a certain seal of approval and confirmation that he had performed well and had the thumbs up from his fellow officers. He drove home at peace with the world. He thought he was like any other man—who had done a good job at his work.

He took the long way to his apartment, just to keep with the feeling he got sitting behind the leather-wrapped steering wheel; holding onto and sensing every nuance of the car dominating the road, and responding to every command transmitted by the driver. Man and machine synchronized perfectly together

Back in his apartment, he opened the last Lone Star from the fridge and turned on the TV; nothing interesting. So, he pulled up recordings of Blue Bloods, his favorite TV show. Toby began to lose himself in the interactions of the idealistic family that had dinner together once a week then went out and caught the bad guys, the prosecuting-attorney daughter who put them in jail, if the oldest son didn't kill them first. The segment ended with the father and daughter having dinner in a fashionable Irish restaurant, the youngest son on a date with a totally wholesome girl he just helped out of a jam and the older son on his way home to his wife and kids.

Sure, it was make-believe, and not realistic, but it dealt with the challenges of life in any large city and the good guys won. It was his favorite show. He turned off the TV and went to bed. Tonight, there was no speeding cars, squealing tires, or gun shots. There was just restful, battery-charging sleep.

CHAPTER 8

TOBY WOKE UP LATE, AND had to hurry to be on time for the eleven O'clock counseling session. Before he left the house, he got a call from Sgt. Ron Perry; his most-favorite training officer. "Hey kid, I hear you're going in for the mental, thumb-screw-treatment today."

"Thanks for the call Ron, but I don't think it will be that bad. Many of the guys have given me good words and I know it was a good shoot."

Ron paused, and then said, "Toby, I want you to pretend I'm still ridding with you and training is still going. What you know and what the top brass thinks can be two different things. And when the smoke clears; what they THINK is the only thing that matters. What you want to guard against is letting them become so convinced in their thinking, that they totally ignore what you *know*. Do you follow me?"

Toby's brain was having trouble adjusting to this suggestion of a conflict between him and the command structure. Was this just coming from the normal tug-of-views between rank and file and management that existed in any organization?

Toby said, "Ron, I really appreciate your call and your concern. You've always given me wise guidance and I'll bear this in mind today, while the brain screws are on. You're a great mentor and I appreciate you. I Gotta go."

As he left his apartment and headed out toward the Camaro, Toby stopped and dropped some coins in the paper box by the parking area and pulled a copy of the morning *Plainfield Gazette*.

The headline and a third of the front page was all about Toby and the aftershocks of the two-day-old burglary and shooting.

He scanned the story and the accompanying photo of him that must have come from personnel. It had been taken when he graduated from the Academy. He had that deer-in-the-head-lights look on his face and he thought the paper didn't do him any favors with that image.

Downtown, he had to wait for the counselor to finish an appointment and he took the time to read the whole story. Ninety percent of the article dealt with the shooting. The reporter had researched and made a point of how few police shootings had occurred in the history of Plainfield, Texas; all twenty years of it. The rest of the story focused on Donald Lindsay and how badly he was injured and how long before he would walk again.

Somehow, the reporter missed the nickname "Bones." The stimulants he used daily that had eaten his body away, leaving a rack of bones, covered by thin skin populated by pocks and sores that frequently oozed fluid from the opened places.

Toby re-scanned the article and his thoughts flashed back to the call from Ron Perry.

"What you know and what the brass thinks—may be two different things. You have to make sure that the brass doesn't become so sure of what they *THINK* that they totally ignore what you *KNOW*."

Toby's thoughts were interrupted by the voice of the receptionist advising him they were ready for him.

CHAPTER 9

THE NAME "DOCTOR JEREMY MONTGOMERY" was printed on the many plaques that adorned the wall. The plaques were awarded from different schools and universities and they all boiled down to the fact that Doctor Montgomery had achieved an impressive set of credentials in the field of psychiatry and had extensive experience with police work. The doctor pointed him to an over-stuffed leather chair that faced another identical chair.

The receptionist brought a glass of ice and a bottle of sparkling water. She sat them on a small table that established a neutral zone between the two chairs; kind of a 38th parallel, DMZ Zone, like in Korea, Toby thought. The Doctor came around his desk and sat in the opposite leather chair.

"Officer Roberts, I want thank you for coming by to see me today. It might be helpful if I go over the procedure we will follow today and sort of put you at ease about what we want to accomplish during our time together. Doesn't that sound like a good way to start?"

Toby said, "It sounds fine to me, I have never done anything like this before so I'll just follow your lead."

"That should be just fine," said Doctor Montgomery. "To start off, why don't I call you Toby and you can call me Doctor Montgomery. Are you OK with that?"

Toby didn't care for Doctor Montgomery's manner. It seemed contrived and patronizing, but he figured that it went with the job description. He resolved to be positive and just get this process done with.

Dr. Montgomery spoke, "Toby, you just said you had never done anything like this before. What did you mean, the shooting or this interview?"

"I've never done either, before," Toby replied.

The doctor began asking Toby to describe the events leading up to the shooting.

"My partner, Sonny Montgomery, no relation I assume, well, he and I were cruising through the parking area at the mall when we got the call from dispatch of a silent alarm at Harold's Drugs. We proceeded to the location with lights and alarm running."

Toby recited the chronological chain of events leading up to and including the shooting with occasional interruptions from Dr. Montgomery.

When Toby was finished, the doctor said, "Describe for me, how you spent your time during the two days following the shooting. I'm interested in your thoughts and your feelings".

"Well, the first day, when I finally got home and tried to get some sleep, I had some trouble at first but I went off to sleep after, maybe fifteen minutes. I did have some dreams about cars coming at me and squealing tires and the sound of gun fire. I woke up a couple of times but then went right back to sleep and finally slept good until my girlfriend woke me ringing the doorbell. I called all my family to let them know I was okay and then I took a drive to relax".

Dr. Montgomery interrupted, "Did you drive to any place specifically while you were on your drive?"

Toby: "Yeah, I stopped at The Precinct, a restaurant and bar, for just a few minutes. I had one beer and left."
Dr Montgomery: "Did you see anyone you knew there?"
Toby: "Well yeah, I ran into a couple of cops who were there when I walked in. I sat with them while I drank my beer."

"Who paid for your beer, Toby?"

"The two other guys had a tab running. They put my beer on their tab."

"How many beers did you have?

"Like I said, just one, then I left and drove home"

"What time was it when you got back home?"

"I don't know, I took a round-a-bout way, it was a while."

Dr. Montgomery leaned forward in his chair, "Toby, you haven't touched your water. Why don't we take a five minute break, drink some water, and relax. I'll be right back after I make a phone call."

He went out to the front office and pulled the door closed behind him. Toby drank some sparkling water and tried to relax, while thinking back on some of the warnings he had gotten from Ron Perry and the cops at The Precinct.

When Dr. Montgomery returned, the questions shifted to how he felt right after the shooting and how he had phrased his words, when he described the incident to relatives and other cops.

After the session with Doctor Montgomery ended, Toby was relieved to be back in the Camaro, where his self confidence slowly returned. Out of habit, he headed toward the precinct station house. A barbeque stand across the street, offered relief from the hunger pains in his stomach; he went in, grabbed a stool at the counter and ordered a pork sandwich and a side of baked beans. Two officers were sitting in a booth near the back; one of the men was Toby's precinct CO, Lieutenant Frank Adams.

Adams was facing the counter where Toby sat and he gave Toby a short nod of recognition and went back to his conversation. Toby had just begun to work on his late lunch when the two policemen stood to leave. Toby saw the two gold bars on the other officers' collars and as they approached, Toby stood and prepared to shake hands. The captain pushed past him without a sign of recognition. Lieutenant Adams paused and spoke in a terse voice, "Roberts, I think you are on administrative leave, what brings you down here today?"

Toby was momentarily thrown off but finally said, "I just met with Doctor Montgomery and came down to have lunch.

Lieutenant Adams half turned to leave and said, "That's fine Roberts, but I don't want to see you in the precinct until tomorrow, and when you arrive, report to my office."

The two officers left without looking back; Toby looking after them as they crossed the street and entered the precinct building. He thought about the encounter and wondered why the command officers were so unfriendly to him when the rank and file seemed so supportive. He got in the Camaro and drove to his folks' house. He needed to talk to *at least* one friendly human being before the day was over.

At Mom and Dad's, he spotted Dad on the riding mower, just finishing the yard and he waited till the mower was stored in the small shop near the back of the property. He and Dad went into the house and Mom came into the kitchen.

"Toby, what a nice surprise come sit down and I'll get you some lemonade," she said. "What nice thing brings you out without warning? Are you hungry?"

"No mom, I am definitely not hungry but the lemonade sounds good. Dad, what are you doing at home in the middle of the week? I didn't expect to see you until the weekend."

"Working on a small center in Abilene, Toby; I can do much of my research and due-diligence from the house. I'm using the phone and the computer this week instead of the airlines," said his Dad. The three settled around the kitchen table where his parents wanted to hear all about his experience over the last few days.

CHAPTER 10

IN THE MIND OF CLARENCE Summers, of all the right things he and the City Fathers had done since the City of Plainfield was incorporated, the crowning jewel was Sky View Country Club and its eighteen-hole golf course. Shortly after he was elected mayor, he had been approached by a handful of the city's most affluent and influential citizens with the idea. It was the perfect opportunity for Clarence Summers to slide into a position of being a partner with the upper-tier section of Plainfield's movers and shakers.

The golf course had been designed by Arnold Palmer's company and was challenging to most golfers in the area. Mayor Walker and 29 of the city's leading and most wealthy citizens had incorporated and arranged the financing. They had no trouble selling the memberships necessary to begin construction.

They hosted one of The PGA Tour matches every year in May and the festivities surrounding the event were one of the top social occasions of the year.

That had been three years ago and as he sipped his martini and waited for his dinner guest, Mayor Summers was mulling over the possibility of running for a second term. He enjoyed the roll of making crucial decisions that affected the lives of half a million people. The pomp and social pageantry that surrounded the job was like that of an addict getting his regular fix of cocaine. The authority bestowed on him, brought a social conscience that he was careful to attend to. Yes, he and the other city fathers had a responsibility—not only to the citizens of Plainfield, Texas—but it extended to the greater population of the metro area, and he thought, even the whole State of Texas.

Mayor Summers had developed a good working relationship with the chief of police, and they tended to generally agree on matters of policy regarding the administration of the police department. In fact, after he took office, he and Chief Cameron Walker had selected a blue ribbon committee to review and re-write the rules of conduct; used to judge the behavior of personnel in the execution of their duties.

The new rules were a great relief to Mayor Summers. He was not a student of police departments, but his instincts alerted him that he needed a precise set of rules to fall back on—whenever the behavior of anyone caused him to judge the right or wrong of the situation. In his way of thinking, bold decisions based on long held values and principles, were highly overrated.

Such a situation may be developing over the shooting that had occurred on Monday, when a young patrolman had shot a man as he was coming out of a store in the northeast area of Plainfield. He had received two or three calls already, from a community-paper reporter, hungry for a story with legs; something he could write about over and over, while making a name for himself. This could be a ticket to a job with one of the big boy's in Dallas or Ft Worth.

Clarence Summers purpose tonight, was to get a confidential report from Chief Cameron Walker—on what his analysis of the procedures manual concluded about the actions of the two police officers involved in the shooting.

Chief Walker entered the dining room and the maitre-de escorted him through the lounge area, back to Clarence Summer's table, in a secluded section overlooking the eighteenth hole of the golf course. Walker attracted attention as he walked smartly through the tables. He was wearing his uniform, decorated with an array of brass and ribbons right up to the four gold stars on each shoulder, and gold braid spread across the bill of his hat.

"Good evening Chief, thanks for giving up an evening with the family. I'll try to make it up to you with a good dinner and not keep you late," said Summers, "I'm sure you have your hands full at headquarters. That's why I thought it would be better if we got together after hours, where we can relax and have some privacy. I want you to be completely candid with me regarding this unfortunate shooting incident. As you are aware, I am up for re-election next year. It is most important that the voters perceive the city—and specifically the police department—as prompt in investigating the behavior of your officer's and whether or not they follow department policy when deciding whether or not to use deadly force."

Chief Walker decided to join the mayor in having a drink before dinner and at the urging of the mayor and the waiter, said he would try the martini.

While the waiter went for the drinks, the chief leaned forward and in a low voice, said, "Mayor, I want to assure you and the council that no time was wasted after the shooting before I ordered Internal Affairs to open a file on the two officers involved. A preliminary report was handed to me this afternoon. I stress the fact that it is 'preliminary' and intend to treat the information confidential until all the facts are brought out. All the information, thus far, indicates the two young men are dedicated professionals."

The Mayor raised his hand and said, "I'm not as concerned with their dedication; it's the public's perception of their behavior in this specific occasion. I have had more than a few calls from some pretty important citizens of Plainfield, expressing their concern that we not get a reputation of being a wild-west town where our police officers shoot first and ask questions later. It's equally important—that our police patrolling the streets of our good city—not develop any Wyatt Earp complexes. Do you get my drift, Chief?"

"I definitely do Mr. Mayor, and I assure you, we will be diligent in our investigation and always sensitive to the image of the city." The chief was already wishing this meeting was not happening.

The rest of the evening went pretty smooth. The chief reminded the mayor he would be going to a conference of mayors in Washington, D.C. next month and while he was there, he and a delegation of other mayors were going to meet with the area members of congress, to remind them of the continuing funding of the many programs taking place in cities all across Texas.

They finished their meal and Mayor Summers was so pleased with the exchange he and Chief Walker had performed, he ordered two brandies, fresh coffee, and toasted the meeting as an example of cooperation, that would surely serve the city of Plainfield very well.

"It won't hurt the careers of a mayor and chief of police either," Summers said and both men chuckled knowingly as they drank to the toast.

CHAPTER 11

WHEN TOBY ARRIVED AT THE precinct, he followed his orders and went directly to the lieutenant's office. He waited outside until Lieutenant Adams finished a phone call, and then he was waved into the office and directed to one of the two chairs facing the desk. Adams was in his high-back, chair, tilted back in a position of assumed authority.

"Roberts, I wanted a word with you before you get back in the routine. At this time, there doesn't appear to be any information that would preclude you going back on duty and resume your patrol. The initial report from the incident investigator—has no red flags but you need to be aware that Internal Affairs will be contacting you to arrange one or more interviews to fully ascertain the true facts regarding the incident last Tuesday morning. I.A. is assembling all the reports; you should hear from them in the next few days. In the meantime, keep your nose clean and try to stay out of trouble, OK?"

At first, Toby wasn't sure how he should respond, but he just said, "Sure Lieutenant I'm always trying to keep my nose clean, but sometimes circumstances seem to bring trouble, when you're wearing blue and brass."

Lieutenant Adams straightened his chair and leaned forward, "Roberts, I have always been pleased to have you in my command and thought your future with the department looked pretty promising. You're a smart young man and could work your way up the chain fairly quickly, but I caution you to not treat lightly, the situation you are in. I will do what I can for you, but I warn you that you are under the magnifying glass. Your attitude and the appearance that you're taking this incident very seriously will be critical to your emerging from this thing in one piece. Cooperate with I.A.D. but never forget—you are your own best friend."

Toby left in a daze. Why were so many people treating him as if he had a contagious disease, when just a few days before, they had begun to treat him as a regular, in what was admittedly a tight fraternity. He went downstairs and found Sonny Montgomery waiting.

"I've got the car ready out back. You can pick up your gun at the property window and we're ready to roll. Time's a wastin' and the bad guys are gettin away," Sonny said with a mischievous smile that suggested he wasn't feeling the same apprehensions that were weighing down on Toby.

They started their patrol, and the routine was soon re-established between them. Toby began to slide back into his comfort zone. He and Sonny talked about things pretty much like they had a week ago. Sonny talked about going water skiing on one of the nearby lakes while he was on administrative leave. He met a new girl in the group and thought there might be a possibility or two with her. He was as normal as if nothing had happened.

They pulled a car over for having a busted tail light, and determined the driver was not DUI. Sonny wanted to just give him a warning, but Toby thought about an audit of the patrol and ticketed the guy. 2:00am finally rolled around and they returned to the precinct. They wrote the report for the shift and said goodbye until later that day at 6:00pm—when they'd do it all, again.

Toby felt restless so he headed the Camaro west on 183 then turned north at Euless and followed the winding road through Grapevine—out to Grapevine Lake. He parked, got out and sat on the car's front fender and looked out at the moon; low in the west, reflecting off of the still water. Toby couldn't shake the foreboding feeling that had returned after the shift ended. He moved to a grassy area that sloped down to the water and stretched his body until he relaxed, and dropped off to sleep.

A light was trying to penetrate his eyelids. The harsh voice kept repeating the question. "Why, why, why didn't you wait? Why did you shoot so quickly? He opened his eyes a crack and saw the light was the sun just peeking over the hills, east of the lake. He stood, brushed off his uniform, and got in the car and headed home. He stopped on the way and picked up breakfast at a Mickey D's near his apartment. He re-heated the pancakes and sausage in the microwave, wolfed it down, and lay across his bed. For a fast food place, he thought they made a pretty good pancake. Maybe, it was just that sleeping on the ground in the cool night air had wetted his appetite to the point that anything would have tasted good.

While his body worked on the sausage and pancakes, he drifted back to sleep. This time, there were no visions or voices to interfere, until the phone ringing pulled him up and he mumbled a sleepy, "Hello." He didn't recognize the voice on the other end of the line.

"Hello, is this police officer Toby Roberts?"

Toby awoke, "Yes, this is Toby Roberts, who's calling?"

"Officer Roberts, this is IAD Officer Lieutenant Coombs, Lieutenant John Coombs. I'm calling regarding the shooting incident involving you, officer Sonny Montgomery and a civilian; Donald Lindsay in the early morning hours of last Tuesday".

"Yes, what can I do for you, sir?"

"You can meet me in interrogation room "B", at your precinct this afternoon at four o'clock. That will give us plenty of time before you report for your shift at six."

"Sure, that time works for me. It will be good to get this thing over with," Toby said.

The voice on the other end replied, "It's a little soon to talk about it being over with, Officer Roberts. We'll see you at four."

The apprehension crept back into Toby's gut. He decided to do his laundry and clean his apartment. Maybe, that would cheer him up a little. At least the activity would take his mind off IAD and a clean apartment always made him feel better.

CHAPTER 12

THE CLOCK IN THE DASH indicated he had about fifteen minutes before his appointment with internal affairs. The traffic was light as he drove toward the Precinct. The Camaro purred like it was happy to be on the road. He loved that about the car. It was happiest when it was performing the tasks it had been designed to do. That's the way Toby felt about being a policeman; he felt best when he was on patrol, assuring the peace for the law abiding citizens and opposing those who attempted to break the peace and create havoc.

Toby parked the Camaro in back and went into the precinct building. Lieutenant Coombs was at the coffee machine making an automatic latte. He offered Toby one but Toby said he was fine and they went into the interrogation room. Coombs closed the door, and they sat, facing each other on opposite sides of the 3X6' table in the middle of the small room. The legs of the table and the chairs were bolted to the floor. A pair of hand cuffs on 3' chains were bolted to the underneath side of the table on Toby's side and an ankle cuff with the same length of chain was welded to each of the legs to Toby's right and left. Thankfully, the Lieutenant didn't move to fasten any of the cuffs to Toby as he sat down.

"This is a formal process we follow, so whenever I address you, it will be as, Officer Roberts," said the IA Detective.

"That's fine, whatever the rules are will be okay for me," said Toby.

"Alright then, Officer Roberts, I want to start off by informing you that my questions to you today will, in no way reflect any opinion or judgment on my part. Our purpose, here, is to help you sort through any emotion you may still be reacting to and get to the truth of what happened in the early morning of Tuesday, March 15, 2011. To make sure we are accurate in these proceedings, we will be recording the questions and answers. You have a bottle of water; is there anything else you need before we start?"

"No, I'm fine. Just go ahead and start."

"Do I have your permission to make a recording of this interview?" the IAD Officer asked.

"Sure," Toby shrugged, "it's fine with me."

The IAO opened a three-ring binder and turned a cover page. "Now, officer Roberts, where were you when dispatch called you regarding a 1011 in progress at 607 Tarrant Street?"

Toby said, "My partner and I were just finishing a sweep of the parking area and access doors at the Prairie Mall."

IAO: The reports indicate it took you seven minutes to drive to Harold's Pharmacy. Is that correct?

Toby: The GPS estimated seven minutes and I gave that to dispatch, I believe the actual time was just over five minutes. That time of night enabled us to make better time than the average.

The IAO read some of his notes: Did you consider handing the call to another patrol, which might have been closer?

Toby: No sir, we were the only patrol in that general area, that time of night and it was in our patrol area, so there was no reason not to take the call.

IAO: Had you ever responded to a 1011 before.

Toby: No sir, I have only been on patrol one year and 1011s don't happen every day in that area.

IAO: So, you were happy to get the opportunity to work a 1011?

Toby: I wouldn't put it that way sir, but it's fair to say that an opportunity to deal with a 1011 would add to my over-all experience level and make me a better police officer.

IAO: OK, let's talk about what happened when you arrived at the scene. How did you approach the premises?

Toby: We did a silent, dark cruise-by, past the front of the store on Tarrant.

IAO: What did you observe?

Toby:	We'll sir; we didn't see much of anything. In fact, it was what we didn't see that convinced us the silent alarm was probably not a false alarm.
IAO:	Can you explain how you knew at that moment you probably had a real 1011 in progress; from not seeing anything?
Toby:	Yes sir, the store was supposed to have a security light burning 24/7 near the pharmacy counter to light anyone up that would be active in that part of the store. There was no security light burning when we made our pass.
IAO:	What did you do next?
Toby:	We went up Seventh and turned slowly into the alley to check the rear of the building.
IAO:	What did you observe from the alley officer Roberts?
Toby:	The back door was opened slightly and a shaft of light was coming through. I figured a light must be on in a storage room by the back door. Then, we saw someone moving around in the back room.
IAO:	How did you approach the back door, to determine what was going on inside?
Toby:	We didn't sir. I called dispatch and reported the situation and asked for back-up.
IAO:	How long did it take back-up to arrive?
Toby:	. . . I'm not sure sir. They estimated four minutes but two minutes later, we saw the intruder come out of the store and put a bag of some sort in the back seat of his car. I think I forgot to mention that the motor of that car was running all the time we were there.
IAO:	Then what happened, Officer Robert's?
Toby:	I decided we couldn't wait for back-up and let the man get in the car. We lit him up and ordered him to stop what he was doing and put his hands on top of the car.
IAO:	Did the man comply with your request?
Toby:	No sir! He dived into the front seat and started driving the car right toward me.
IAO:	Were you still near the patrol car? What did you do?
Toby:	No sir, when I got out of the car, I had crossed over to the far side of the alley, to my left from the squad car. Officer Montgomery had moved straight ahead of the squad car on

that side of the alley; standard formation when approaching a suspect. As the guy kept trying to aim the car right at me, I was trying to go back to my right toward the squad, but he kept turning toward me. Honestly, Lieutenant, it's a miracle I'm still alive. The headlight missed hitting me square—by less than an inch. I felt the curve of the fender push against my leg and hip, and then against my butt, as I twisted hard to my right. It was only a second later that the open door smacked me on my left shoulder, almost knocked me flat but somehow I stayed up.

IAO: Where was your gun while all of this was happening, officer?

Toby: In my right hand sir, I had drawn it when I stepped out of the car.

IAO: Am I to understand that up to this point you had not fired your gun?

Toby: No sir, there wasn't time, sir. I was scrambling to keep from getting run down.

IAO: What did you do next, Officer Roberts?

Toby: I raised my gun and fired ten shots at the car, sir.

IAO: Were you aware of any other shots being fired at the same time you were firing your gun?

Toby: No sir, I was not aware that my partner had fired his gun until later.

IAO: You mentioned that you were busy trying to avoid being run over. Did I understand that correctly?

Toby: Yes sir.

IAO: Then after you had avoided being struck by the car, did you still consider yourself under attack?

Toby: Yes sir, I suppose I still thought of myself being under attack.

IAO: Well Officer Roberts, I think we've covered all we have time for today. According to the clock on the wall behind you, you have fifteen minutes to freshen up and report to roll call. I'll notify you of our next session in a few days. Just a reminder, you will still be under oath when that occurs. That will be all for today; you're dismissed.

CHAPTER 13

T HE NEXT FEW DAYS PASSED without any incident. Toby and Sonny were getting back into the groove. Sonny had sat through a twenty minute interview with IAD and was advised that no further questions were anticipated. Toby was puzzled by the thought that his session had lasted an hour and he was waiting for the call scheduling a further session. What else was there to talk about, he wondered?

The local newspaper had run the initial story on the Tarrant Street shooting—*as it was now referred to*—and two follow-up articles about how many police shootings were occurring across The United States. A local Unitarian Pastor was quoted as saying that the elected officials and top brass at the police departments around the Dallas/Ft. Worth area should exercise more supervision and review; and do a better job of training their new police officers.

The paper concluded the article, with the pastor's words, *"We are already involved in unnecessary wars in foreign countries. We certainly don't want war breaking out in the streets of American cities."*

Toby glanced over at Sonny, "What do you say, want to meet up Sunday morning and go over to The Unitarian Church for a little spiritual guidance?" They both had a good laugh and felt better as they started their patrol.

It was Saturday, about 12:30am when they responded to a call from dispatch regarding an altercation at the *Silver Spur*. The *Silver Spur* was a country/western saloon and dance-hall. They turned on the lights and siren and arrived two and a half minutes later.

There were two entrances into The *Silver Spur*. On one side—the door led into a large, open area where there were tables and chairs arraigned in a semi-circle around a large dance floor. On the other side—the door opened into a smaller area, containing a large bar that extended two thirds of the width of the room and was shaped and decorated to look like a horse shoe. Toby and Sonny entered on the bar side and observed two bartenders; one on either side of the curved structure, taking care of about twenty to thirty, thirsty cowboys. A huge back-bar, fully stocked with every kind of booze a cowboy could want, formed a colorful display on the counter in front of a plate glass mirror that reflected every ugly son-of-a-bitch sitting at the bar. One of the bartenders met Toby at the back side of the bar, while Sonny walked behind the cowboys at the middle of the curved bar.

"Good evening officer, I think we may need some help with the extra-large one with the long red hair. He's been here all night and when I refused his last order, he got pretty mad and started wanting to fight everybody at the bar. When I tried to calm him down, he reached across the bar and punched me in the mouth before I could duck; fast, for such a big mother, he is." There was a little trickle of dried blood at the corner of the bartender's mouth.

"Are you OK," Toby asked?"

"Yeah, I don't want to make serious trouble for him, if you can just get him to leave," the bartender said as he dabbed his mouth with a damp bar towel.

Toby turned toward Sonny, and nodded toward the big redhead, who was now in a loud exchange with a man on the stool to his left.

Sonny stepped to go between the two men as Toby came up on the right side of the redhead.

Toby said in a friendly voice, "Alright, buddy, what do you say; about ready to call it a night? Come on and we'll help you outside, these guys are about ready to close up and I think you've had enough for tonight."

The redhead collected his focus and slowly turned his head until he was starring into Toby's alert blue eyes.

The man's mouth curled into a snarl as he said, "Fuck off, little boy blue." He started to laugh at his own words.

"Listen pal, we can do this easy—or if you insist—we can make it ugly." Without warning, the redhead came off the barstool while grabbing Toby's uniform shirt and lifted him up to where his toes were barely touching the floor. Behind the redhead, Sonny was raising the wood nightstick that he brought from the car. Without hesitation, he swung it full force, striking the large man just above the right ear. The stick made a loud cracking sound and broke in half.

Toby could hardly believe that through the assault, the man shook his head to detour the blood running from the gash left by the stick, but barely loosened his grip on the front of Toby's shirt. True to academy training—about the importance of gaining control and not allowing uncontrolled violence to spread among a large number of civilian's—Toby pulled his 9mm from its holster and pushed the end of the barrel deep into the fat of the man's stomach and pulled back the hammer. The clicking sound from the hammer managed to get through the music and the whiskey that was powering the man's reflexes, and he froze.

Toby spoke in a near whisper, "Now, you son-of-a-bitch, take your hands off of my shirt and put them on top of your head. Sit back on the stool. My partner is going to put cuffs on you and if I see any effort to resist him, I'll put so many holes in your bloated-gut they'll have to bury them with you in a garbage bag. Do you understand? Just nod your head cause I don't want to hear your voice!"

They called dispatch and waited for the EMTs to patch the gash above the redhead's ear and look at the bartender's split lip. Then a paddy wagon showed up to haul the guy to the hospital for a check-up.

"Probably couldn't have fitted him into the back of your squad even if he wasn't hurt," said the driver of the paddy wagon. "He's one of the biggest I've ever hauled. Good work fellows, see you later."

They drove back to the precinct and spent the rest of their shift writing a full report of the encounter and then Toby drove the Camaro to his apartment.

Toby lay in bed a while and thought about how tame the first year on the job had been and wondered if this was the preview of the future or just a fluke of incidents pushed close together. Either way, he felt good about how he had reacted in both instances; the drug store when he had used deadly force, and tonight, when he'd only threatened it. He drifted off into a dreamless sleep.

CHAPTER 14

I T WAS GOING ON SEVEN, Thursday evening. The Texas sun had settled down for the day, but a persistent breeze, moving five to ten miles an hour was pushing north and bringing extra humidity from a weather system in the western end of The Gulf. Houston had been suffering from the same system for a couple of days and was now generously sharing the warm, humid air with the DFW Metroplex.

Troy Taylor was driving the mid-sized Buick, he had checked out of the city's motor pool. He had driven the car around to the side door of city hall and waited until Clarence Summers had finished a meeting with the director of public works. When he finally came out to the car, it was a close call, whether they would be late for dinner with The Council of Concerned Clergy. The Clergy was a small group, four men and one woman, who were constantly going around with their finger on the panic button; ever-ready to sound the alarm on some wrong that they wanted somebody to make right. Usually the city fell into the "make it right" group.

Troy's full time job was being a financial planner/stock broker for *W.R. Jones and Company* but was now serving his third term on the city council and this year he had been elected president of the group. It was an honor that Troy coveted because it indicated the ability he had demonstrated to find consensus on sticky issues and bring at least a voting majority to a decision. It also was another item on the list that he might present to the local Republican's for support in seeking a seat in the Texas Legislature, in the future.

In Troy's opinion, this little group meeting tonight was a motley collection of left wing activists, with a social, guilty-conscience a mile long. He knew they were going to complain about the shooting by the two young officers. In Troy's opinion these young officers should be getting medals instead of accusatory questioning by the IAD.

Troy glanced over at the mayor and said, "Tell me Clarence, what is your honest opinion of this group we're meeting for dinner. Do we take them seriously or just pat them on the head and move on?"

Clarence thought for a couple of seconds. "Troy, I learned a long time ago that groups like this one are like a boil on your butt. When it starts, you barley notice, but it slowly gets worse and you scratch it. It then gets infected and you wind up at the doctor's office, he lances it and puts a big bandage on it and then you wind up at home where you have to eat your meals through a straw while lying on your stomach. All this could have been prevented, if you had gone to the drug store and bought a bottle of liniment, and treated the problem while it could have been controlled."

"So, are you saying these people are like a boil on our butts?" Troy asked with a smile.

"More like a pimple that we don't want to become a boil," Clarence mused, half to himself.

"So, I take it you are not fundamentally in disagreement with the conduct of the two officers Roberts and Montgomery on the night of the burglary."

Troy, the biggest patch of quicksand in government for men like us is the police. You can't operate without them and quite often, you can't live with them. I'm afraid a large portion of people in our community would not condone shooting of a burglar, no matter what he had stolen."

"I get that point, Mr. Mayor, but I don't think we can forget that the burglar tried to use a car to run our officer down and potentially kill him."

"I understand that argument but he didn't kill him, did he Troy? I have had a briefing from John Coombs, in IAD. He says they are going to do further interviews with the officers; particularly Roberts and he will keep me in the loop. Yesterday, I had a brief visit with the city attorney. Rodney Dawson says that Roberts may have violated a city rule on the use of deadly force when he fired his gun as the burglar's car was going away from him. According to our administrative rules, IAD contends, once the car passed Roberts, it was no longer a threat and at that moment Roberts was forbidden the use of deadly force."

Both men gave way to silence until they arrived at *Ropers Restaurant*, a quiet family favorite with a small, private, dining room in the back of the main area. The five concerned clergy were having coffee and waiting when the two walked in and began shaking hands and greeting their hosts.

After he finished his dinner, Mayor Summers pushed back his chair; "Gentlemen and Lady, I thank you for the fine dinner and the opportunity to become better acquainted with each of you and hope you have gotten to know us a little better. It is through this type of encounter that we are able to come together and find the balance that works for all the citizens of Plainfield. We have had a good exchange while we were eating, but at this time, if you have specific questions that I can address, feel free to ask."

The lady pastor of the Plainfield Unitarian Church said, "Mayor Summers, I think all of us here are anxious to know how you are going to discipline the officer that recklessly fired a dozen shots at a burglar, and risked the lives of any residents who might have been nearby. We wonder if your police department is trained to think they have a right to end someone's life before they are even found guilty of committing a capital—crime."

Mayor Summers scanned the people at the table. "Thank you for your very blunt question. I also like to get right to the heart of the issue. I'm sure you all understand that this is a personnel matter where the city is concerned. There are certain laws that govern how I and President Taylor here, and the rest of the council deal with such matters. While the rights of the two officers will be strictly protected, I can safely assure you that their conduct in this matter will be strictly measured against the law and the department rules that spell out the procedures that are and are not permitted."

Another fifteen minutes and they were able to gracefully excuse themselves and leave.

Troy Taylor drove in silence for a few minutes then said, Well I think you handled that group pretty well. I don't detect any boils in that group." He chuckled at his humor.

Clarence Summers stayed quiet for a while then spoke. "You have to look below the surface of the ocean to see the wave that will tear sand out of the beach a minute later. We must keep an eye on the lady minister and not let her build too much momentum." Then turned toward Taylor, "I'm glad you came along tonight, Troy. You may have helped to blunt their charge a little, but we must be cautious. Try to remember the exact words that she used when asking her question. I don't think we've heard the last from the lady.

CHAPTER 15

TEXAS HAD NOT ALWAYS BEEN bold in its financial commitment to the field of public education. The state and consequently local communities had erred on the side of controlling state and local budgets in order to hold down taxes. In most ways this policy had succeeded in attracting new businesses that provided a steady supply of well paying jobs and relatively happy taxpayers.

The citizens of Plainfield had made an exception to this practice when they decided to build a new high school. Sam Houston High was going to be a physical monument to the belief in the city's future roll in educating the young men and women that would shape and direct the future of the best and brightest that Texas would follow and prosper from. It was big; in the truest definition of Texas Big.

The school was built in three structures connected by covered walk-ways in a loose triangular pattern. In some ways it gave off the feel of a miniature college campus. "Sam Houston" as it was commonly referred to by 450 students and their parents, was intended to be a fountain of learning for its students. It was their home away from home, five days a week and open Saturday mornings until noon for independent studies and research by serious students.

The typical population of the Sam Houston on a Saturday was 150-200 students. Not everyone was inside cracking the books. Some were lounging at various locations where chairs and benches were placed so one could enjoy the pleasant view and receive what stimulations and inspirations might be escaping from the three impressive buildings on all sides.

Edward Sandusky was not receiving any random stimulation from the campus as he walked deliberately through the scattered students, heading straight toward the middle building. In fact, Eddy Sandusky had never been able to open his mind to the flow of information that even the average student received from the classroom. School had always been like a foreign country to Eddy. He wanted to be there but found trouble with the language and the culture. He just couldn't find the fit. The long sports bag in his left hand did not contain basketballs or tennis racquets as its shape suggested. Eddy was not there for a pick-up game with some buddies. In fact, Eddy didn't attend Sam Houston and didn't personally know anyone who did.

Eddy Sandusky didn't attend any school and hadn't for at least three years. He had been aware of the project, when Sam Houston was under construction. He had fantasized for a time that he would attend the big school and be one of the little rich boys that thought themselves better than everyone else. Eddy hated being put in the part of the community these little pricks looked down on.

His last try at school had ended when a teacher expelled him from her class for her students from study and causing serious injuries to three of those students by striking them with a piece of a chair that he had broken against a wall. The principal had made some phone calls and arraigned for Eddie to report to another school that specialized in handling problem students. Eddie never reported to the special school.

Eddy had gravitated to the skid row area of Dallas. For the next three years he lived on the streets and at the houses supplied by distributors of the drugs to which Eddy had become addicted. Eddy also worked as a recruiter for the supply of boys and girls to the human slavery markets. Working the bus station, train depot, and the periphery of the middle schools located in the poorer districts, produced his best results. When his recruiting efforts were unsuccessful, Eddy became part of the supply chain. He loathed the dirty men who used him as their sex toy and imagined that all their kids attended Sam Houston while he catered to their dads and uncles. Most of the afflictions that assailed Eddy were, in his clouded way of thinking, because of the snooty kids that attended schools like Sam Houston.

Eddy had prepared well for this day. Two of the guns had been obtained from a home burglary two weeks ago. They had been an unexpected bonus from an effort to get some small electronic appliances that could be sold or traded on the street or pawned at one of the less scrupulous pawn shops in Dallas. The guns had started him developing the scheme of how to perform the job ahead—at this place, against these people. Yes, they would all remember Eddy Sandusky and regret their treatment of him. Once the scheme formed in Eddy's mind, the rational justification, or lack of it, never occurred to him.

As he approached the middle building which he knew housed the library—where the stupid, spoiled brats would be pouring through their fancy books filled with lies. Today, they would face their judgment from Eddy Sandusky.

As he came to the steps leading into the building, Eddy reached into a side pocket of the long, canvas bag and retrieved the long-barreled target pistol. It was a .22 caliber automatic with an 8" barrel and he had loaded it with fifteen .22 caliber magnum-ammunition bullets. Another pistol was in the side pocket, but it was a small framed .38 revolver made in Czechoslovakia. That would be good for taking out anyone that tried to stop him from making his escape. The rifle in the long section of the bag was a beauty; a military issue 9mm, with an 18 shell magazine of pure killing power. Yes, they were going to know Eddy Sandusky, after today.

A student was approaching Eddy as he took the first step up toward the front entrance and called to him, "Hey dude, the gym is in Building A. Are you new here?"

Eddy raised the target pistol and pulled the trigger twice, striking the young man squarely in the chest. He was dead before his body hit the sidewalk. Eddy continued up the stairs and entered the doors without looking back.

In the hallway, two girls were standing at a locker laughing about a story that one had just told the other about a boy they both knew.

Eddy walked directly to them, a smile on his face. The girls paused and looked at him, trying to place the face.

"Hi," one of the girl's spoke, and before another word, he shot her through her left temple. An instant look of terror in the eyes of the second girl as she saw her friend sway toward the opened locker and then crumple to the floor. She turned away to flee down the hall but the second shot hit her in the back of her head and she fell defenselessly forward, her face striking the tile floor, just after the super propelled bullet exploded through her forehead.

In the library, the shots in the hall were unmistakable and a seventeen year old boy opened the door to investigate. Another shot roared from the hall and the frosted glass pane in the door exploded. The student pivoted back into the library and began to run away from the door. Eddy pointed the pistol through the opening in the broken glass and shot the fleeing boy in the back. Five shots, four down; it was going to be a good day, thought Eddy.

Now he opened the damaged door and entered the library. Panicked students were running in all directions and screaming incoherently. Some were hiding under tables or desks but others were simply running. It was like a shooting gallery at the county fair, thought Eddy, as he methodically selected one moving target after another. Yes, their fathers and uncles would be sorry they ever messed with Eddy Sandusky.

Down the hall, Martha Downey, a fifth year teacher was preparing Monday's lesson for her history class while she monitored the building for the Saturday seekers of knowledge. She heard the first shots outside the building and wondered if it was a car backfire. Then, when the next two shots were fired, she thought GUNFIRE? HERE?

She stepped to the window and saw what appeared to be the body of a young boy, lying on the sidewalk near the front steps. The body was on its back and the legs were twisted backward, in an unnatural position and not moving. A feeling of unbelievable horror swept through her and her first instinct was to run out and render aid. Instead, she ran to the phone and called the police.

CHAPTER 16

TOBY WAS JUST WAKING UP and hadn't yet climbed out of bed when the police scanner crackled. "All units, shots fired at Sam Houston High school. Witnesses report wounded on the outside of Building A and shots have reportedly been fired inside the building in the vicinity of the hall and the library. All tactically-assigned units proceed to the campus and assist the SWAT that is en-route to the scene. Tact-trained officers off duty check in to your precinct for instructions.

Toby's phone rang and Sonny's voice said, "Hey, I was out in the car when I heard the call. I'm near your apartment; I can swing by and pick you up."

"OK, I'll call the precinct for instructions and meet you out in front of my apartment."

Five minutes later, Sonny screeched into the parking lot and Toby jumped in the car.

"Precinct says we should go directly to Sam Houston. We won't worry about uniforms but we need our necklace badges and an arm band, so we don't draw friendly fire," Toby said as he put on the seat belt.

I have a spare gun in the glove compartment," said Sonny, as he glanced over and saw Toby was wearing his Glock.

They arrived at Sam Houston five minutes later. Sonny pulled in behind the scattering of squad cars and he and Toby made their way over to the big SWAT truck. They grabbed four arm bands—red with large black PPD lettering. A sniper would not mistake them for the perp. They hoped that another officer would have the same observation powers and take time to make the right call before taking a shot.

SWAT had a floor plan for the building, which showed doors on the front and back and a door on each end leading to the nearby buildings. One additional door was a fire escape door in the back wall of the library. Fire codes had dictated it because of the size of the room and the large number of students that might assemble there at one time. Toby, Sonny, and two uniformed officers were assigned to the two back doors. Toby and Sonny took the fire escape door coming from the library, positioning themselves behind two trees about thirty feet from the door.

The lieutenant in charge of SWAT dispatched a team of eight heavily armed marksmen in black camouflage suits. "We're still hearing shots coming from the library. I want the son of a bitch that's shooting put down quickly before any more kids die. We've retrieved three bodies; one near the front steps and two girls in the hall with head wounds, all fatal. This guy is here to kill people; make sure none of you are one of his kills today."

As the inside team approached the door to the library, another shot rang out inside followed by a quick volley which sprayed the wall near their door. They could not see the shooter but the team leader heard through his sound amplifying head-phones, the shooter curse and jacked the breach of his rifle for more bullets. Then he heard the gun clatter as it fell to the floor. The lead man pulled the door open and one by one the team went through the opening, alternating left—then right, running in a crouched position.

The third man through the door spotted the shooter as he opened the fire door. He fired while on the move and saw wood splinters fly from the door frame. He thought that at least one of the shots should have found its mark but the man went on through the door to the outside. There were loud voices outside the door then two shots followed by many shots. Then it was all quiet, except for the sounds of groans and cries for help from the wounded.

The SWAT leader went to the fire escape door and saw the body of the shooter lying about ten feet from the door and two officers; out of uniform with large badges strung around their necks and PPD arm band's just above their elbows. Each was holding a smoking 9mm Glock and walking toward him.

It was Monday Morning and Mayor Clarence Summers was pacing a tight pattern behind his desk—between the flags of the state of Texas on one side and the stars and stripes of The United States on the other. He paused at one corner of the massive desk and grabbed his cup and drank a gulp of black coffee. It had started with Sunday's paper which ran headlines proclaiming "TERROR STRIKES AT SAM HOUSTON HIGH." The first paragraph recounted the number of dead and injured students. The next paragraph named the assailant and detailed his troubled past as best they could, since much of it was protected by the laws dealing with juvenile misdeeds being kept confidential.

A separate article with a smaller headline read, "*PLAINFIELD COPS TRIGGER HAPPY??*" The article started, "*Toby Roberts and Sonny Montgomery, recent additions to the Plainfield Police Department have raised questions in the DFW area regarding the guidelines provided policemen governing their use of deadly force in the performance of their duties. These two young officers have been primary officers in two incidents in less than sixty days in which one civilian was shot twice, and is expected to suffer from the wounds the rest of his life, and the juvenile assailant Saturday at Sam Houston High School, whom the same two officers shot multiple times resulting in the death of Edward Sandusky, eighteen. Mayor summers, Chief of police, Cameron Walker, and key members of the City Council could not be reached for comment—.*"

Mayor Summers sat the cup down and turned to the police chief and council president and said, "Damn it, Cam, can't your line officers get these two green recruits under control. The paper has the knives out for us and if you don't deal with this problem, the voters will be right behind them."

"I understand your concern Clarence and I assure you I am on top of the problem but you can't forget, we are bound by state law, city ordinance, and departmental regulations when we deal with matters such as this," said the chief. "By the way, let's not forget, we had a building full of terrified school kids getting killed like clay pigeons—which every cop out there was trying to save. Maybe we need to pin a medal on these two officers, instead of letting the press and the PC Patrols put us in a panic. And, let's not forget our agreement with the Texas Police/Patrolman's Association. They may not be as powerful as a union but I don't think any of us want to go to war with them," Troy Taylor said. "Some of us are up for re-election in just about 16 months."

Chief Walker stood to leave, "Well, the two patrol officers will be on Administrative Leave for the next three days. By then, I'll have all the details. You'll both be kept fully informed as we go along."

CHAPTER 17

THE DFW METROPLEX IS BIG even by Texas definition. It occupies over 9000 square miles of land and water; 95% of it being land. It is home to 6,371,000 widely diversified souls, each pursuing his or her personal agenda, and many following their own rules.

The story of two rookie cops trying to do their job in Plainfield might be classified as a "tempest in a tea-pot" to the officials and leaders in Plainfield, but it had not even appeared on the radar screen in either one of the two large cities that dominated the Plex.

The situation at the "Petroleum Community Bank and Trust" of Dallas, fairly reflected this fact as the officers and staff busily focused on the needs of their depositors and borrowers this Monday morning.

The manager, Paul Broderick had arrived at 7:00am, as usual, and had gone directly to his office to review two loan files that he would recommended approval on at the meeting of the loan committee, later today. The bank, true to its name, catered primarily to the oil and gas industry and the investors that funded the never-ending search for more energy. The two loans being approved today were not large by the banks standards but the borrowers were regular and highly valued clients and he wanted no slip-ups at the meeting.

Lucy Thompson, the chief teller, and four other employees arrived at 7:30am and began to get things in order to open at 9:00am. It was an hour earlier than most banks opened but most of their customers were busy business operators who needed access to their bankers as early as possible, and PCBT did not want another bank to be tempted to supply this convenience to lure those demanding clients to move down the street.

Lucy was blonde, in her late thirties, and took good care of herself. She was 5'9" and had a good figure; which she worked on at the health club three nights a week after work. She had no children from her failed marriage of seven years and was not currently dating anyone. Her life was without conflict and her salary from the bank provided all the comforts, and a few luxuries, she spoiled herself with when she pleased.

The time-locks activated at eight o'clock and the tellers began to set up their stations, ready to open. Paul Broderick asked the chief teller to open the doors at 9:00am so he would not be interrupted from the loan files.

When Lucy Johnson went to the front door, she was a little surprised that there were already six customers waiting. She didn't recognize any of them but, after all, the bank had thousands of customers and no one could remember them all.

Lucy unlocked the large doors and wished them all a good morning and they filed in and went in various directions. The first man walked toward Mr. Broderick's office and the other four went toward the teller windows. When Lucy finished, she went to her desk at the end of the teller's row and noticed one of the men waiting there.

Lucy walked around her desk and sat down. "Good morning sir, how can I be of service?"

The man had a large briefcase in his lap. He turned the case toward him and opened the lid. When his hand came up, he was holding a large gun pointed at Lucy. "You can sit still and keep your mouth shut until I say you can talk. Keep your hands on top of your desk and don't move your feet to trigger any alarm. If I think you are trying to signal anyone, I'll shoot you dead. Nod your head "yes" and smile if you understand."

Lucy nodded her head and saw Paul Broderick and a man walking toward her desk. She glanced to her left and saw all four tellers starring straight at each man at their windows, as if in a trance.

Paul Broderick came to her desk and said, "Lucy, bring your keys and come with me to the vault. Do not try to resist these people in any way. What they want is money and it is not worth getting hurt to try to stop them."

As Lucy stood she saw that the tellers were placing their cash in plastic bags. Then she followed Paul to the vault and tried to ignore the gun that was jabbing her in the back.

The man behind her leaned close and whispered in her ear, "What's wrong bitch, don't you like being poked in the back by something hard. You look like you need to be poked with something hard and I might decide to do some serious poking while I'm here. You'd like it, I guarantee."

The other man overheard the taunt and scolded, "Flint, knock it off and keep your mind on what we're doing here."

In the vault they emptied the cash lockers in the front, then forced Paul and Lucy to use their combinations on the dual-locked door to the rear half of the vault and finished filling the large bags they had brought folded in their brief cases.

As they finished, Flint came up behind Lucy and reached around her with his left hand and began to fondle her left breast. It happened so unexpectedly, it startled her and she jumped away from him, slapping at his hand. He swung his right hand intending to hit her with the gun. When the gun struck her, he squeezed the trigger. The sound was deafening to the people in the vault; but not to Lucy. To her, it sounded far away and as she felt herself sliding toward the vault floor, everything seemed to fade to black.

After the shot was fired, the other man in the vault yelled, "Flint, you stupid bastard, I told you to leave the woman alone. Now look at the mess we've got. Pick up the bags and get out front before I shoot you and leave you here."

"You go to hell, Turk. I was just having some fun and the bitch hit me."

Turk put the barrel of his gun in Flint's ear and spoke in a flat un-emotional voice, "If you don't pick up the money and get the fuck out of this vault, I'll kill you right here and leave your sick ass for the cops."

Immediately after the shooting, the six hold-up men grabbed the bags of money and, one by one, went to the side door and disappeared out to the street.

Paul Broderick ran to the front of the vault and pushed the alarm button. Then he ran to the nearest phone and dialed 911. In less than one minute, sirens were approaching the bank from three different directions. The EMTs were three more minutes arriving. There was a large pool of blood around Lucy and her face was unrecognizable. The first assumption was that she was dead but Paul had received training for this kind of event. He reached for her wrists and felt a faint pulse. He knelt by her, covering her with his suit coat, and began applying pressure with his handkerchief against the ugly wound across the side of Lucy's head and face, speaking words of encouragement to her until the police arrived.

*   *   *

The University of Texas' Southwestern Hospital rated over and over as the best hospital in Dallas. The team of surgeons was always busy and this morning was no exception as they operated on Lucy Johnson. In fact, the surgical team working on her now was the second team assigned to Lucy since she arrived at 9:41am, today. The first unit had stopped the hemorrhaging and restarted her heart twice.

The team of specialists, working in the trauma unit now, were attempting to give her brain room to swell and make repairs to the wound left by the bullet which had entered above her right ear and extended downward and deepening till it tore through the side of her mouth and took bone from her chin.

Lucy hadn't regained consciousness—that was a blessing in the minds of the surgical team. In fact, they were now keeping her in a coma until they could get her condition stabilized.

No one in the bank or on the street witnessed the get-a-way vehicle but it was assumed to have been waiting at the side door. Six men in the bank, and presumably, a wheel man in the waiting car, plus six bags of cash needed space. An All-Points-Bulletin (APB) was issued describing the six men through the Metroplex Alert System (MAS) with possible types of vehicles. But, at nightfall, they had not received a single report of any suspicious group or vehicles.

A Captain and a team of police, including four detectives and six uniforms, were assigned to the case; Lieutenant Douglass Freeman, Lieutenant Charles Gorman, Detective 1st Grade; Jorge Rodriguez and Detective 2nd Grade; Paul Chan. All four were seasoned veterans with an impressive file of tough cases and arrests that stood up at the DA's office. Two FBI Agents met with the team and all agreed on a division of responsibilities.

The six uniforms were assigned computers, searching the internet and all social media sites with key words for clues. The two detectives went to the phones, contacting every snitch they knew—or knew about—to start the awareness process to spread through the streets. Someone, in the shadowy world that existed between the criminal and law enforcement layers of society, might provide a tiny shred of information that could point the police toward the bank robbers. The two lieutenants organized a command post and the system to process and eliminate leads until a picture began to develop that would lead to an arrest.

The first few days were frantic but when no solid leads were produced, everyone settled into the monotonous routine of following their training and experience which took over their long days and nights.

Then the gang struck again. This time they entered the main branch of Southern Commerce Bank, in Ft. Worth. The method was the same: come in at the opening and control the bank employees, strip the teller stations and empty the vault. The descriptions matched up with the robbers in Dallas, at Petroleum Bank. The robbery in Ft. Worth was a carbon copy of Dallas with one exception; this time one of the tellers dropped a bundle of bills that fell to the floor. The robber, apparently, mistook her movement as an attempt to push an alarm and shot twice, killing her instantly.

A team, almost identical to the one in Dallas, was assembled in FWPD and one member of the team was assigned to the task of liaison with their counter-parts in DPD. Two days later, The FBI and the Chief's of Dallas and Ft Worth held a joint news conference and announced the formation of a task force led by the Bureau. Every cop in the Metroplex was now on alert for the gang of bank robbers.

The Chief of both police departments pledged there would be no rest until this band of outlaws was brought to justice.

CHAPTER 18

Toby Roberts and Sonny Montgomery were just two of the thousands of police who were very conscious of the hunt for the gang that, in police circles, was being referred to as Turk and Flint's gang, referring to the names spoken in anger by two of the robbers. All efforts to match the names locally or through the NCIC (National Crime Information Center) had been unproductive.

Meanwhile, Toby had been re-interviewed by IAD Officer, Lt. John Coombs. This time Coombs focused in on Toby's own statement that he had fired every shot from his weapon, after the car had missed hitting him and grilled him about the car not being any further threat to Toby at the time he fired his weapon.

Coombs had asked, "Officer Roberts are you familiar with department regulation number R-251 which specifically sets limits on the use of deadly force by an officer of PPD?"

Toby had replied, "I believe it states that an officer shall not use deadly force against a suspected felon while running from the officer while attempting to make an arrest."

Adams continued, "From all we know and from your own words, Roberts, that is apparently, exactly what you did, didn't you?"

"I don't think that reflects my situation, lieutenant. I believe I was defending myself against a lethal attack by a man using a deadly weapon," Toby retorted testily.

"Well, Officer Roberts, we'll see whether what you believe carries more weight than command's interpretation of their rules of conduct." Coombs stood and left the room.

*　　*　　*

The competition that developed between the speculations, over Toby's shooting and the theories on the two bank robberies, was pretty intense. Not that it was important, what the rank and file in all the uniforms in the Metroplex thought, but there was never a lack of something to talk about when two or more officers were together, particularly in places like the precinct lounge.

Sergeant Ron Perry had just ordered a second round for his table of new recruits. They had just completed a final phase of their training and he was continuing the long tradition of christening the start of a proud career with two beers.

One of the young officers spoke, "Sergeant, I was told that you were the training officer for Toby Roberts, the guy that's in trouble over that shooting at a drug store a few months ago."

"Yes, that's correct, I am proud to say that Officer Roberts was one of my prize students."

The young officer continued, "I'm surprised you're proud of the guy. From what I hear, Roberts is a real cowboy; out of one scrape and into another. Did he learn his tactics from you or was he that way when he came aboard?" The young officer was trying to impress Ron Perry that he had access to information not normal to the run-of-the-mill recruit.

Ron Perry swallowed some of the fresh, cold beer, leaned over the table, and spoke in a confidential tone, "I don't know what you boys think you know. I don't know who, you think you know, but you're about to get some straight talk and advice. If you remember the talk and follow the advice, you just may—and I emphasize 'may—have a long and successful career with the Plainfield or some other police department. Part of my training is to prepare you young men to avoid approaching a perpetrator with a know-it-all, cocky attitude and winding up dead on the street with a smirk on your face." Perry continued, still leaning close to the two young officers, whose eyes were now opened a little wider, "I just said I don't know who you think you know, but I'll tell you now, you don't know Toby Roberts and neither does whoever fed you the misinformation about him or Sonny Montgomery. What you don't know is that Toby Roberts went to college to learn how to be the best police officer he can be. He flipped hamburgers for almost two years, waiting for an opening in Plainfield PD because he thought we had the best organization to finish the job that his college education had started. He got out of the precinct and onto the streets, and found that things weren't as simple and clear cut as his professors and other politically ambitious men would have all of us believe. So he wound up shooting a couple of scumbags and scaring the shit out of a third. If you two are half as professional and use half the good judgment that Toby Roberts has shown in just over one year, we may come back here a year from now and have another beer. If not, I will probably be attending your funerals in less time than a year."

Perry leaned back in his chair and drained his bottle, "Now, you boys can go on and have yourselves a good evening. Don't enjoy yourselves too much because, tomorrow, I'm going to be on your asses just like I have been for the past two months. Stay out of trouble, you hear?" Ron Perry walked out of The Precinct without looking back.

*　　*　　*

It was twelve-thirty in the afternoon and the wait-staff at *Carrington's Restaurant* was just clearing the last of the dishes from lunch in the private dining room. Emily Rodgers stood to call everyone to order and begin the program. Judy Rodriguez sat at the head table to Emily's right and was ready to hand the engraved, crystal trophies to their two guests. Toby Roberts and Sonny Montgomery were sitting at the first, round table, in front of the head table with the podium and microphone, which Emily Rogers now clicked on and tapped to make sure it was working.

Emily was the wife of Calvin Rodgers, President, CEO, COO, and every other job necessary to make International Bureau of Investigation stay busy, out of trouble, and profitable. So far, Cal Roberts had succeeded in all categories and enjoyed a well thought of reputation with most all the Police Departments in the Metroplex. Judy Rodriguez, wife of Police Detective Jorge Rodriguez, was an active leader in the Hispanic community and had made the transition to the greater community when she had been elected vice president of Concerned Citizens for Public Safety (CCPS). Today marked a first for the organization toward accomplishing their announced purpose: "To encourage and recognize the extraordinary efforts by law enforcement officers and citizens toward protecting and ensuring the safety of our population."

The crowd of 58 attendees turned their attention to the head table as Emily Rodgers began to speak, "Ladies and Gentlemen, it is with a special sense of pride, that I move us into the business part of our meeting today. This is an opportunity to move our purpose of existence from words into action. I've had the privilege and rewarding experience of having the opportunity to become acquainted with—and get to know a little about—the young men we are honoring here today. I don't believe we could have found two young men more deserving of our recognition than these two outstanding officers. Most of us are unaware of the pressure we put on our police officers in a major population area like our Dallas, Fort Worth Metroplex. We spend extensive resources, training them to perform tasks that are often in direct conflict with each other; protecting the law-abiding residents from people who would do them wrong, assisting in conflict resolution between the best and worst of us, and sometimes forcibly restraining those bent on using violence against us and against the police, themselves."

"Recently the two young men we are honoring here today, encountered, what we might call, a Perfect Storm of events that called on them to exercise all their training, skills, and even their ability to restrain themselves from the full application of their abilities. From the tragic and senseless slaughter at Sam Houston High, to a store robbery, to a bar fight, we owe these two men our deepest and most sincere thank you for a job well done." So, without further delay, I'm pleased to call on our Vice President, Judy Rodriguez to come forward and make the presentation to Toby Roberts and Sonny Montgomery, our "Community Protector" award recipients, for their outstanding service."

Judy Rodriguez stood and walked to the microphone. "It's a distinct pleasure for me to second the remarks you just heard from Emily. As the wife of a Dallas Police Detective, I know first-hand the stressful conflicts that follow these men that go out every day and try to balance the rights, guaranteed to us all by our constitution, while assuring the safety of most of us—against the assault by a few. These two young men have demonstrated they have the training and skills to make the split-second decisions, which deliver that balance. Officers Toby Roberts and Sonny Montgomery, we at CCPS proudly recognize your excellent service with this award."

Toby and Sonny stepped to the front of the room and accepted the awards and the enthusiastic applause. The reporters and photographers were there from three newspapers and two TV stations. It was a heady moment for the two but they soon made their excuses and slipped out to get ready for work.

In the Camaro, Toby said, "Well partner, I hate to say anything about it but I think you may have to go back to the uniform store and get fitted for a bigger hat. I'm sure your head grew two sizes during lunch." Toby laughed. Sonny smiled and gave Toby the middle finger salute.

CHAPTER 19

C HIEF CAMERON WALKER AND ASSISTANT Chief; Ralph Wiggins were preparing to commence a meeting with Lieutenants Frank Adams and John Coombs from Internal Affairs Department. The only civilian present was Rodney Dawson; City Attorney. The pressure was building from an ever increasing number of so called civil rights groups, and the anti-gun crowd and one or two groups who were, basically, anti-police. Chief Walker had called this meeting to get out ahead of the growing cries against Officers Roberts and Montgomery. He anticipated another visit from Mayor Clarence Summers and the rest of the politicians up for election next year. They wouldn't be there to discuss the right or wrong of the conduct of the two officers. Rather, they would just want him to reassure them that come election time; the voters would not hold them accountable for the actions of Roberts and Montgomery.

The mayor began. "Let's get started. John, why don't you and Frank bring us all up to speed on the assessment you've made based on your interviews with the two officers."

Coombs said, "I think I'll have Frank begin with the information he has discovered from his interviews with the two and the investigations to verify that information."

Frank Adams cleared his throat and began. "I have interviewed both officers twice and am pretty clear on the sequence of events from their recollection. I have also interviewed the back-up team that arrived about two minutes after all the shooting took place. I conducted one interview with the wounded man, Eddy Sandusky, in the presence of his court-appointed attorney. Not much there, I'm afraid. I, also, have statements from the EMTs that responded and the crime scene team. Boiling it all down, I have a pretty clear picture of what happened and when."

Chief Walker said, "Why don't you give us a summary of that, lieutenant."

Adams looked at John Coombs for a signal and continued. "The procedures followed, by Roberts and Montgomery, as they made their approach and sized up the situation at the drug store, were handbook correct. Their communications with dispatch were complete and informative. When the individual came out of the store, the two officers could not see, clearly, what he was doing. They thought he was about to get into the car, which would make the job of detaining him to determine his activity more difficult. They made the decision to light him up and stop him from getting into the car."

"Is that when all hell broke loose?" Rodney Dawson asked.

Adams resumed, "It is my opinion that the sudden lights, combined with Officer Roberts' command over the PA, to stop and put his hands on top of the parked car, panicked Sandusky into jumping into the car and attempting to leave the scene. Tire marks in the alley seem to support Roberts' story that Sandusky tried to run him over but narrowly missed, brushing against him with the fender and then striking him on the left shoulder with the opened door on the driver's side."

The mayor was leaning forward and asked, "What happened next?"

Adams said, "Roberts realized he was still holding his gun, a Glock-9MM with a 12 round magazine fully loaded, and he began firing. He fired ten shots at the car and struck Sandusky twice; once in the left shoulder and once in the left leg, just below the hip."

"What was happening with the other officer, Montgomery?" asked Rodney Dawson.

Adams went on, "Montgomery, at first, thought Roberts was injured and was running to check him out and see if he could be of assistance. When Roberts began firing, Montgomery joined in, firing his gun twice."

City Attorney Dawson walked to the window and looked out. "I'm not a policeman but from a purely legal stand point, I'm at a loss to find any wrong doing on the part of these two cops."

Coombs picked up a thick binder and said, "Regulation 151." He smiled as he tossed the heavy bound book on the table.

Dawson looked inquiringly at the imposing book of documents, "What the hell is regulation 151?"

Coombs went on, "Regulation 151 in the department's operating manual prescribes when deadly force may be used and specifically some occasions when deadly force may not be used. One occasion when its use is not allowed is when a suspected felon is running away from the scene of a crime and is not posing a threat to police or civilians. By his own testimony, Roberts confirms that Donald Lindsay was running away from a crime scene and was not posing a threat to anyone at or near the crime scene when Roberts fired his gun."

"Is there a difference between running down the street from a liquor store with a broken window and the alarm going off, and leaving the scene of a silent alarm in a car and trying to run over a cop who has ordered a hands-up and stand-down to a perp?" asked Rodney Dawson.

Chief Walker turned in his chair, "It depends on who you're asking. A patrolman on the beat will have a different opinion on that question than an ACLU Attorney or The Council of Concerned Clergy. I have an opinion, when I am just wearing my cop hat, but my job comes under the auspices of the Mayor and City Council and as much as we wish it was different, politics plays a big roll when issues like this comes into play."

There was a smattering of small talk and, one by one, each man went off to their respective offices mulling over the implications of what they had discussed; and what had not been said but had occupied their thoughts. The three cops struggled with the double standard implied during their meeting while the city attorney was more at ease with the reality of the role that politics played when dealing with the tough issues that faced them and government officials and law enforcement people at every level all over the country. Everything had become so political, it wasn't easy to keep straight about what was right and what was wrong. It was always the question of how would their decisions affect the next election.

Fuck the politics and the gutless politicians thought Chief Walker, as he entered his front office. "Gladys, check my file and see how much time before I can retire." He went through the next door into his private quarters.

Gladys smiled sympathetically and went back to her computer. She had no problem understanding Chief Walker's growing interest in retirement.

The pressure kept building. All the area newspapers ran daily articles with different slants on the two officers in Plainfield, with endless speculation on their competence and what their treatment would ultimately be, along with articles criticizing the lack of any progress on an apprehension of the gang of bank robbers.

CHAPTER 20

"TOBY, BRING THE PLATTER OF steaks into the dining room and let's sit down to dinner," Toby's mother called out.

Toby was getting a beer from the fridge.

"And if you're getting yourself a beer, bring me one," said his dad.

It was Sunday and Toby had the day off. He had spent most of the day at Karen's house watching The Cowboys beat the Jets.

"Why didn't you bring Karen out to dinner, Toby?" His mom asked. "I really like her, and I think she has been good for you."

Toby smiled. "Thanks, Mom, I really like her too but we are taking things slow and easy. She needs to be alright with my job and before she can be sure about that, she needs to be sure how she feels about us."

"Is there some doubt there?" asked his Dad.

"It's not a matter of doubt, Dad, as much as confirmation of how she thinks she feels; how we both feel."

His mom took his hand. "You don't need to feel any pressure from us, Toby. I know what you went through before with Sara. You both seemed so much in love and thought that was all that mattered. Then when Willy was shot and killed by someone he had just pulled over on a traffic violation . . . that just panicked Sara, with the realization that a policeman faces so much danger, even in situations that we don't think of as dangerous."

Toby pulled his hand free from his mothers grip. "I know Mom, and I don't want to go through that emotional experience again with Karen. Don't worry about it. We're doing fine. We enjoy one another's company and pretty much like to do the same things. Things will work out for us, or they won't."

His Dad spoke from the end of the table, "She's a Cowboy fan and that makes her alright in my book. Pass the potatoes."

Everybody was busy filling their plates, and then Toby's Dad held his hand up and said, "Before we eat, I want to thank God for blessing us with three good sons and for keeping Toby safe."

After dinner, Toby helped his mom pick up and carry dishes back to the kitchen. He gave her a hug and told her, "Mom, I don't want you to worry about me. Not me and the job—or me and Karen. I feel good about what I'm doing and I believe my personal life is going to fit just right with my profession."

Toby hugged and kissed his mom and headed for the door. His dad walked him out to the Camaro.

"Thanks for coming out tonight, Toby. It is very important to your mother and me that we see you and talk to you in person. I have to admit, I'm as concerned as Mom about how you're really doing. I don't mean with Karen; I'm confident you'll work that out. I'm concerned about the job. You've had three episodes recently, anyone of which could have a lasting effect on your conduct when you run into similar situations in the future. I'm, at least, apprehensive about whether some other scum-bag might hurt you because you hesitate to use appropriate force the next time you're in a similar situation."

Toby put his hand on Darrin Roberts' shoulder. "Dad, I love you and Mom and I understand the concern. I have thought a lot, in the last few weeks, about the events that caused me to make instant decisions about whether to use my gun on those people or let them decide if they were going to kill me or not, and I assure you I have no regrets about the actions I took. What I know, and you need to understand, is that I have had thorough training that anticipated each of those events and prepared me for the action I needed to take. I took appropriate steps in each case and I can live with the results. If the politicians and top cops play politically correct games with what I did, I can't control them. If I had to face the same situations today, I'd do the same things, except, maybe I'd shoot a little sooner at the guy trying to kill me with a car."

Darrin Roberts looked his son over carefully, then reached out to him. As he embraced Toby, he said in a low voice, "Toby, you've really grown into the job. Don't worry about Mom, I'll assure her that our son has his head screwed on straight and we can sleep easy, knowing he's got us covered. I don't, completely understand your comment about shooting sooner at the drug store."

Toby spoke as he got in the Camaro, "Nothing for you to be concerned about, Dad, but there is a little regulation in the Department that says that an officer may not use deadly force on a suspect that is fleeing the scene of a crime. If Sandusky would have been running away from me, down the alley, I don't think I would have fired on him. But, I reacted to him attacking me with his car and even though he was headed away from me when I fired, in my mind the attack was still in progress and I was defending myself against further efforts. IAD and others seem to be hanging their hat on that regulation and interpreting it differently."

Nothing more was said, except goodnight, but as Toby drove away, both men were deep in thought about the issue.

CHAPTER 21

THE NEXT DAY, TOBY WAS off duty. He slept late and when he'd finished breakfast, decided to clean his apartment. The phone rang in the afternoon. Sonny wanted to know if he was planning to attend the meeting of their chapter of the Texas Police/Patrolmen's Association. He decided, sure why not? Sonny said he would swing by and pick him up.

On the way to the meeting they talked shop and speculated on what it was going to take to catch the gang of bank robbers.

"They're probably laying low," Toby said, "they've taken over $700,000 in the first two jobs, according to the banker's statements."

"Yeah and we know those figures are always under-stated," Sonny replied.

They arrived at the Sheraton and found their way to the conference center where the meeting was just getting under way. They each grabbed a bottle of water and an agenda and found seats near the back of the room. A few men had recognized Toby and said hello and some came over and shook hands and gave him a thumbs-up signal.

The agenda was long and soon became monotonous and boring. Toby got up and walked to the rear of the room near a small group that seemed occupied in serious exchange on a subject unknown to Toby. He took another bottle of chilled water and when he turned around one of the men in the group turned and walked to him.

"Hi, they tell me, you're Roberts. I'm Lieutenant Perez; just call me Skip. How are they treating you, Roberts?"

Toby looked the man over carefully. He was slight in build but looked strong; about 5'10" in height and Toby guessed he would weigh-in at 190 lbs. of pure muscle. He was all Hispanic, with close cropped black hair, and black eyes that never stopped looking at everything that moved around him. His smile was disarmingly friendly, but Toby saw an icy-coldness creep from the back of the smile.

"Yeah Lieutenant, uh . . . Skip, good to meet you, I'm still reporting for my shift and they haven't taken my badge away so I guess I'm staying ahead of them. I haven't met you before, what precinct are you out of?"

Perez looked Toby over, "Right now we are working out of the 3rd, but we're all over the place. I've heard your story and to be honest, I've read the reports on the three incidents that have made you famous recently, and when you have time, I'd like to buy you a drink and find out your version of these adventures."

Toby was embarrassed at first but sensed a serious purpose in the lieutenant's suggestion. "Lieutenant Perez, I don't know why you're interested in my problems but I don't have anything to hide and you seem like a likable guy; so, if you want to buy me a beer one of these days, I can go for it. Here's my card, give me a call." Toby spotted Sergeant Ron Perry across the room and walked over to say hello.

Toby reached out to shake hands. "Ron, it's good to see you, how are things?"

Perry smiled broadly. "Fine, Toby, it's going well on my side of town. How are you holding up?"

"Everyone keeps asking me that question, Ron, and I keep telling them that I am just fine."

Perry glanced toward the group that Perez had rejoined and asked, "You and Perez friends?"

"No, were not friends. In fact, I just met him a few minutes ago. He came over and wished me well and then said he'd like to buy me a drink and hear my version of my adventures lately. Seemed like a nice guy. He said he works out of the 3rd."

Perry looked concerned, "Be cautious with Perez, Toby. He walks a fine line that not very many cops can handle; and he plays a pretty tough game with the badge."

"I don't know what you're getting at, Ron. Do you think he's a crooked cop?"

"No Toby, at least not as far as I know, but there are rumors in the rank and file than Perez is a lone-ranger. He seems to make his own rules as he goes along; and gets away with it. I have never known him to have his tail in a crack with command, and I have never been aware of any outstanding record of arrests; kind of glides along in his own stratosphere, immune from the viruses that are constantly attacking us mere mortals."

"You call him a lone-ranger. What does he do? How does he operate?"

Perry hesitated a moment, then said, "All I can tell you Toby, is he has a team of three or four guys and I'm not sure what their assignment is. My guess is they operate, pretty much, under the radar and answer to someone higher up the food chain than the commander of the 3rd Precinct."

Toby stared across the room, "Well, I guess it won't be the end of the world if I just let him buy me a beer. As of today, when it comes to how I'm treated by other cops, he fits in with the good guys; right beside you, Ron."

Ron Perry tapped Toby on the shoulder and said, "You're a good cop, Toby, and don't let anyone make you think otherwise. The system can get pretty twisted sometimes but those of us that are on the front-lines in this war understand that we just have to keep our heads down and our eyes on the bad guys. Leave the politics to the boys with the gold braid on their hats. I'll see you around Toby. Try to stay out of trouble for 24 hours, OK."

Toby caught Sonny's eye and motioned him to the door and they went out to Sonny's truck and left.

Well, I see you and Ron Perry had a chance to chat; what's new with him?"

Toby stared out the window. "Not much, he was just giving me a little fatherly advice . . . I think. You know how it is, once your training officer, always your protector and adviser."

Sonny made a right turn and started up the on-ramp to the freeway. "What was the advice about today?"

"He saw me talking to Skip Perez and seemed worried that Perez might have a bad influence on me; something like that."

"Yeah, I saw you and Perez in a huddle. He has always given me the creeps; I don't know what it is about him but I just kind of feel the hair stand up on my neck when I hear him talk . . . you know, the words come out cold and flat, without any feeling; just makes me uncomfortable."

Toby looked at Sonny and replied, "That's sort of what Perry had to say about him. You two been comparing notes on Perez?"

Sonny turned off the freeway and headed for Toby's apartment. "No, I haven't talked to Ron, but what did Perez want to talk to you about?"

Toby said, "He's been hearing about the incidents we've been involved in and he was just giving me some encouragement. He said he had read the reports and thought we didn't need to feel bad or apologize to anyone for how we handled the situations."

"He read the reports? How does he have the OK to read our reports? He's not in the chain of command where he would have easy access to our reports." Sonny said, half to himself.

"I don't know, Sonny, he's been in the department a long time and probably has friends in records that would let him see a report if he asked for it."

Sonny pulled up in front of Toby's apartment, "It still seems odd he would ask for all three files. The three incidents had very little in common with each other. They were different types of crimes and the only thing I can think of that would be consistent is us having to draw and in two of the incidents, use our weapons."

Toby climbed out of the pickup and said, "I don't know partner; cops are curious by nature and I will probably comply with my curiosity if Perez calls and meet him for a beer. Thanks for the ride. We got another day off tomorrow, so I'll see you Thursday morning at roll call."

CHAPTER 22

THE NEXT MORNING, TOBY WAS getting a slow start. After Sonny had dropped him at his apartment, he'd called Karen to see if she wanted to come over. She said she was just going out the door to join some girlfriends from work and would call him when she got back home.

Toby drove the Camaro to a Tex-Mex drive through and brought home a dozen hot wings and Mexican fries, turned on a recording of *Blue Bloods* and chilled.

Karen called about ten o'clock and they talked for an hour. Toby didn't talk about the job too much with Karen. It didn't seem to bother her when he did, but his past romantic experience had made him more cautious about how much a young woman, not involved or experienced in police issues, could handle. Later, when—or if—they married, there would be time to share the issues he dealt with.

They had said goodnight about 11:00pm. Toby fell into bed and had a peaceful and restful sleep, except the 3:00am trip to the bathroom; too much beer, too late in the evening.

The next morning, Toby had finished breakfast and picked up clothes and started a load of laundry, when the phone rang.

It was Skip Perez. "Hey Roberts, I understand your off today and I thought we might meet at *Big Jim's Burgers and Beer Pub*, about 1:00 and have some lunch. How does that work for you?"

This guy doesn't waste any time, Toby thought, as he said, "Yeah Lieutenant, I suppose I could squeeze that into my busy schedule. I'll see you there about 1:00 this afternoon."

"I'm buying! Perez said, travel light."

Toby finished his laundry and called Sonny. "I'm going to have a burger with Perez at 1:00 this afternoon."

Sonny exclaimed, "Wow that was quick. I don't have a real good feeling about this, Toby. I want you to call me when you're finished and fill me in on the juicy details. OK?"

Toby promised to call Sonny back after the lunch.

*　　*　　*

Big Jim's was a combination: burger restaurant and bar with twenty different ways to prepare a hamburger and an equal number of choices of side dishes, ten different beers on tap and more brands still in the bottle. The main entry area sported a huge salad bar and two tubs of help yourself soups. The place was divided into five different areas, with walls 9'tall, not reaching the 15' ceilings with exposed trusses.

The fifth dining room was the smallest, located in the rear of the pub at the end of a hall that started at the door to the kitchen, having only four small tables, four chairs at each, and one long table set up with 14 chairs.

This is where Toby found Skip Perez, already nursing a tall mug of richly gold colored liquid.

"What brand of beer you going to have?" Perez asked.

"Lone Star, long neck," Toby replied to the waitress who had escorted him back to the small room.

The girl flashed Toby an extra warm smile and said, "You just have a seat and I'll be right back."

The girl turned and demonstrated the correct way to exit a room, especially if you wanted all male eyes to follow until you were out of sight.

Perez had watched Toby. "Nice girl and a damn good waitress. I try to get her at my table whenever I come here. Sit down, Roberts and relax. Are you having a good day?"

"So far, I can't complain", Toby said.

"Well, I'll try not to give you any reason to complain when you leave here", Said Perez.

The girl came back with Toby's beer and asked if they wanted some time or if she should get their lunch started.

Perez said, "Well this guy has the whole day off but I've got to go catch the bad guys this afternoon so we better order.

The girl stood right by Toby's elbow and leaned over twice to point out items on the menu; each time brushing her breast against his shoulder.

Perez watched but made no comment. "I wanted to get to know you better, Roberts. You've had a lot of intense police work thrown at you in a short period, recently. Some cops work twenty years and never draw their weapon; much less fire it. Now, in one month you have drawn your gun three times, killing one, wounding one, and scaring the shit out of a third right in front of his drinking buddies. You are a bad ass motherfucker. You are!"

Toby squirmed in his seat, "I never started any of those days out to be that. Every day I go to work, I intend to protect the good people from the bad. I studied hard at college for my degree in criminal investigation and then again during Academy. It has been my intention to be the best policeman in Texas; and that is still my goal."

Perez leaned toward Toby, "How does it make you feel when the shrinks and the politicians start second guessing your decisions after you have dealt with circumstances that require split-second decisions?"

Toby hesitated and then replied, "I understand they have their job to do so I try not to let their actions and their questions get to me; but I have to admit, it's starting to piss me off. Well, maybe pissed off, is not the right words. I feel a little sad when command seems to be against me instead of supporting me."

Perez leaned back in his chair, "How many times have you replayed the shootings in your mind since they took place?"

Toby looked up, "I don't know, a few times at first trying to get the sequence straight and in the right order. I was thrown a little when the IAD and others started making an issue of my shooting when the guy was driving away from me."

The burgers arrived and they ordered two more beers; which gave the girl two more opportunities to walk out of the room.

When she brought the beers, Perez said, "Toby, if you haven't figured it out yet, the best thing about eating here is not the burgers.

No, the best thing about coming to *Big Jim's* is watching Shirley walk in and out of the room."

Shirley smiled at Toby and said, "This guy is one of my favorite customers and I love all the compliments he gives me. I hope you'll come back real soon. Maybe you'll become another one of my favorites."

Perez said, "Hell, Shirley, the way you've been all over him this afternoon, I'd guess he's already your favorite."

Shirley turned to leave and Perez gave her a pat on the ass as she passed his chair.

Perez turned to Toby, suddenly serious. "Roberts, I've got a question for you. If you were back in that alley behind the drug store and the scumbag refused your order to stop and put his hands on the car and started driving toward you trying to run you down, would you get out of his way and let him drive off?"

Toby didn't hesitate, "No Lieutenant, this time I would shoot before he got to me, then I'd get out of the way."

"That's the right answer, Toby. At least for me, that's the right answer. Now the politicians won't like that answer because it doesn't fit in their little politically-correct handbook and it doesn't sound good at their cocktail parties with their friends with guilty consciences over how much money they have."

"All I've wanted to be for six years is a good cop," said Toby, and I thought Plainfield was the best place for me to realize my goal."

Perez drained his beer. "I think it can be, Toby, we just have to fit you into the right place in the puzzle. I have a few officers that work with me on special projects. We don't go to roll call—we wear street clothes and drive cars that look like they might belong to your neighbor. We don't work regular shifts but when we're on a project we, often as not, work it around the clock until the mission is done. Based on what I just told you, would you be interested in transferring over to my group and helping us catch the bad guys?"

Toby thought for a few seconds. "It sounds pretty interesting, or maybe exciting is the better word. I would like to think it over and talk to my duty officer and a couple other officers I respect."

Perez cut him short. "Toby, I would like to let you do that but I can't. You see, this unit is very special, and moving into it can only happen at my invitation. Your duty officer hardly knows we exist and even your precinct commander knows little about us. If you decide to join us, I have to know your decision by noon tomorrow. If you accept my invitation, your command and duty officers will be notified. I must ask you NOT to discuss our conversation with your partner or other officers in advance of making the transfer. Are we clear?"

"Yes sir, I get the message. How can I call you?" Toby asked.

"It'll be better if I call you. Look for my call about one o'clock."

Toby drove the Camaro at an abnormally slow speed back to his apartment. His thoughts were flying about in a random pattern, despite his efforts to establish order.

He was unsettled over his treatment by IAD and higher-ups in the command structure. He felt a threat to his career ambitions. He didn't mind serving his time as a Patrol Cop; in fact he rather enjoyed the hands-on aspect of dealing direct with the people he was supposed to protect and the element that might harm them. Things were not going according to the plan, and he had felt that for a few weeks. Now, here was Perez seemingly with a get-out-of-jail-free-card; this could solve all his problems with one change in his file and he could be away from all the people who were demonstrating their total lack of loyalty and concern for him.

Toby hesitated to call Sonny when he finally arrived back at his apartment. Instead, he called Karen and they talked over an hour, mostly about nothing in particular except themselves and family stuff. He didn't say anything about his meeting with Perez.

It was about 6:00pm when his phone rang and he answered without looking at the screen. It was Sonny.

"Hey partner, I thought you were going to call when you and Perez finished lunch. Don't tell me you've been talking all afternoon."

Toby hesitated, torn between his genuine friendship for Sonny and a sense of needing to keep his connection with Perez between himself and the gatepost. "No, I'm sorry but after I got back, Karen called and we talked for a long time. I was just going to call you."

Sonny said, "So tell me the juicy details. I want to know all the dark secrets you found out. What did he want? What did he tell you?"

"Not much, Sonny. He mainly wanted to give me some encouragement. He was pretty aware of the tough time I'm getting from IAD and he just wanted me to know that Command is treating me like crap because of politics. He thinks both of us are doing a good job and that was pretty much what lunch was all about."

Sonny said, "Well, that's weird that he would buy you lunch when a phone call would have accomplished as much in five minutes and been a whole lot cheaper. He must have had another purpose in mind. He didn't invite me to lunch."

"Well, Sonny, you know IAD has had a hard-on for me since the drug store shooting. Perez knows about that and I assume that's why he bought me lunch. You are suspicious about his motivations, but I gotta tell you he came off as a pretty nice guy. I'll probably never hear from him again."

Sonny was quite, then said, "Don't kid yourself, guys like him don't do lunch because they feel sorry for some schmuck patrolman. He wants something, Toby; you need to be careful with Lieutenant Perez."

Toby called his folks and found out his dad was on the road. Later, he got in the Camaro and drove out to their house and had dinner with his mom. She was glad to have the company and he felt noble about the good deed. He got back home about 10:00pm, selected an old Mickey Spillane movie from his DVR collection and then went to bed about midnight.

The next morning, about 10:00am, IAD called Toby to schedule another interview to address some "unanswered questions." He made up an excuse about his schedule and asked them to call him back tomorrow.

By one o'clock, when Perez called, he'd decided.

"Lieutenant, if I accept your invitation, will you assure me that my problems with IAD will go away and not come back?"

Perez said, "Roberts, I can make your current hassle go away and if you follow the few rules I have, I guarantee they won't bother you while you work for me. Okay?"

Toby replied, "Lieutenant, you've just increased the size of your unit."

"I thought you were going to say 'yes' and I want you to know I feel real good about the change. You're scheduled for patrol at 6:00pm. I will take care of the change in schedule, so you are no longer on your current assignment. I want you to report to the 3rd, tomorrow at 9:00am. They'll have some minor paperwork for you to sign and then I'll start getting you acquainted with the other members of the team. Just ask for me at the front desk. See you tomorrow, and wear street clothes."

Toby started to pick up the phone and call Sonny—but he checked himself. Perez had been clear about keeping this move quiet until it was done. He would call Sonny tomorrow and bring him up to speed.

THE 3ᴿᴰ PRECINCT WAS IN a mostly commercial area, mixed with apartments and smaller houses. It was the remnants of what was there before the incorporation of the town. Some of the buildings had been renovated; like the two-story one, housing the 3ʳᵈ.

Toby arrived at 8:45am and asked for Perez. The desk sergeant gave him a file folder, told him to follow the highlights on the forms, sign where indicated, and then directed him to a small conference room down a hall to his right.

At 9:00am sharp, he had finished the paperwork and Skip Perez walked thru the door carrying a three ring binder.

"Good morning, Roberts. Are you ready to start to work?"

"Yes sir, Lieutenant, here are the papers I have signed. I think they're all in order.

"Give the folder back to the sergeant, he'll check them. You'll find that I don't do paperwork as a rule, and I don't ask my men to do any more than department rules demand. Now I'm going to give you a brief over-view of my unit and our mission. You are, no doubt, aware of the many repeat offenders that go in and out of the justice system like they were in a revolving door. Some of these are minor offenders that are more a nuisance to the system than a threat to public safety. On the other hand, we have an assortment of more serious offenders that manage to maim and occasionally kill good folks and through the skilled help of smart criminal lawyers, often with influential connections in the community, escape the full impact of the law. The third group that we deal with in our unit—are the smart and highly organized professionals. These scumbags plan their crimes thoroughly, down to and including their escape and destroying evidence that they were ever near the scene of their crime.

Perez stood and asked if Toby wanted a re-fill on his coffee. He left the room for two minutes and came back with two steaming cups.

"How are you doing so far, Toby? As you can see already, the picture is pretty small. It's the interpretation that fills a large book."

"Yeah, I can understand the problem. It's always been there but what do you do about it that we're not already doing?" Toby asked.

"That's the question, Toby, and it has been asked by everybody for many years." Perez was now on his feet. "Guess what, the answer is in our unit."

"What?" Toby asked.

Perez stopped in front of Toby, looked squarely in his eyes, and said, "Everything necessary."

"Everything?" Toby questioned.

"I know I'm hitting you hard with the concept, but I selected you for this job because you have, at an early point in your career, come face to face with the illogical conflict that man inserts into the process of enforcing and prosecuting criminals with laws that are measured against our constitution; at least recent interpretations of our constitution. Governments, at all levels, have been forced to create small clandestine units like ours to do what they will not allow the larger bodies of law enforcement to do in plain sight."

Perez stopped pacing and sat back down at the table across from Toby. "The man you shot and wounded at the drug store has a long record of burglary, armed robbery, car theft, and drug dealing. He is a real scumbag and no one knows how many people have died as a result of his illegal activities. The man you shot and killed at the school, if he had been arrested alive and well, would have been on trial with appeals for twenty years or more—at best; worst case, would have him found mentally incompetent and sent to a cushy mental re-habilitation institution and released in a few years because a group of shrinks decide he's no longer a threat to society. Are you getting the picture, Toby?"

Toby spoke after a while, "It's a shitty situation, Skip. How do we deal with it and not get hanged ourselves?"

"Courage and innovation Toby, and quiet protection by the powers that be." Perez put his hands on the table as a symbol of completion. "What do you say, Toby? Are you ready to join the battle to protect your parents and other members of our community; are you ready to make the commitment?"

"Lieutenant, if you like the way I handle myself on the job, and the people who are beating up on me for what I did will protect me if I do the same in your unit, I think I'm ready to make that commitment you mentioned." Toby reached across the table to shake Perez's outstretched hand.

*　　*　　*

Over the next few days, Toby met the other members of the unit. The men referred to themselves as The Double T's. Each one introduced themselves by a nickname. Tyler, Tiny, Tip, Timer, Tracker—and they had decided to call him TB—if he had no objections. He had none. They offered no elaboration on the names, and he didn't push it.

He spent most of the next few days listening and riding with Perez. He learned they had an impressive network of contacts.

Every cop developed his or her snitches that they could turn to for "street information" (SI). It was like *Facebook*; only in person. The "street" always knew what was happening in the shadowy world of the scumbags. The problem was there was no clearing-house for all the gossip. So, one had to go to various sources to get the straight story on specific individuals and/or activities.

The TTs tried to compartmentalize the areas of intelligence and skill sets they collected so they didn't waste time duplicating one another's efforts. Much of the time, their intelligence was required on an *on—demand* basis. Events created an immediate demand for knowledge that only the *street* knew and they were ready to find out that information quickly and quietly.

The TTs met every two days and had a beer and brought one another up-to-speed on any cases they were working and Perez would brief them on any new situations they needed to add to their alert list.

In the first meeting Toby (TB) attended, they met at *Big Jim's Burgers*. They talked about Toby's shooting victim at the drug store. Tip reported that Eddy Sandusky was healing up pretty quick from the bullet wounds and had been assigned a very sharp and well-connected Public Defender. The PD was making a big deal about Sandusky being shot while leaving the scene of a possible burglary, before any reasonable evidence had been established. There was also some debate about Miranda being executed properly, and a possible deal for a reduced plea and a suspended sentence. The deal was given pretty good odds, since the shooting officer was no longer in the precinct where the arrest originated.

Toby was angry. "That's a bunch of bullshit. I pulled Sandusky's sheet after we arrested him. He has been dirty most of his adult life and had a juvenile record before that and my partner read him his rights while he had him handcuffed to the steering wheel."

All the guys were all smiles as Skip spoke, "Well, TB, you're getting a taste of the frustrations we deal with all the time. If you were still in your old command, they'd pat you on the head and tell you not to worry."

Tyler spoke up, "And with the other hand, they'd slip a blade between your ribs."

Everybody chuckled around the table and shook their heads knowingly.

Skip was making notes in a small spiral book and said, "I'll put it on the watch list, for now. Tyler, you have the assignment to track Sandusky and keep us posted on any deals with the system. We want to know if he's going to walk. Next, Tip is going to catch us up on the bank boys and the Task Force."

Tip pulled a small spiral from his jacket. "No further activity from the scumbags and the taskforce is walking in place. They are poking around but mostly, my source says, they are praying for another attack. They think they're ready for them if they make another move, but they're frustrated by the lack of productivity of intelligence from normal sources. They think their dealing with a whole new gang or at least a new leader. Nobody is trying to move the money on the discount market—that they've detected."

Skip interrupted, "Anyone here picked up any vibrations?"

Tyler spoke up, "One of my bankers reports an inquiry about the mechanics and the legal limits on transferring funds out of the states for foreign investments. The bank officer handling the query didn't get concerned until he got a memo from my friend—and then it was too late. He gave the man a set of rules, and if further inquiries follow, I will get a heads up."

"OK," Skip continued, "how we doing on our friend that likes to hurt women; Tiny where are we on this sicko?"

Tiny referred to his spiral. "Bobby Conway's last victim can't or won't make an ID or give a very helpful statement. She has totally refused to be counted on as a reliable witness. Her husband is a worthless weakling who is blaming her for the rape as much as the scumbag. Her face is pretty messed up. Surgery will help but she will never heal real well. There are two good officers on it from downtown, but they are running into brick walls everywhere. They have given me everything they have, on the "q.t.", it's your call."

Skip asked, "How many priors; any convictions?"

Tiny turned the page. "Total incidents as a suspect—eight, in two years, prior to that he was a 'person-of-interest' in four. The last one of those was attacked in her sleep and never woke up until it was over. She did regain consciousness as he was going out the bedroom window and she scratched him on an arm. She got some skin under her nails and lab got a DNA match from a mouth swab swipe. He did 18 months for burglary on a plea but there was insufficient evidence for the rape. The son-of-a-bitch is clever about cleaning up after and has yet to be nailed for rape. Three of his victims have serious psychological problems and one has permanent kidney damage from the stomping and kicking he did before he left"

Skip closed his notebook and said, "Looks like a failure on the part of the system on this creep. We need to take him out of circulation, any suggestions on method?"

Tiny spoke, "These creeps don't usually tolerate pain very well. If we're just going to disable him, we could castrate him."

A couple of heads nodded and chuckles went around the table.

"Do we have a clear picture of his daily routine and access to him without making a scene?" asked Skip

Tiny nodded, "I've tagged him two different times. It appears our boy is pretty into meth and he goes into a shooting house at 13th and Hopper to get his fix. One night, he stayed a couple of hours but the next time he floated out of the place after 30 minutes."

"OK, Skip said, I want Tiny and Timer on this, and TB, you can get your feet wet on this one. Tiny, you decide on the time and place. Timer, you get a special car and pick up your team when Tiny gives you the go. Tiny will identify the bum when he comes out of the meth house and signal TT that he's the target. Timer, you're the wheel man. Make it a clean hit and run. The cover story to the investigating team is one druggy running over another druggy. Take the car to a chop shop and they'll make it disappear in an hour."

Skip stood and raised the remains of his beer. "Good meeting gentlemen. If we keep chipping away, we'll definitely see the improvement out there. See you in two days, unless you hear different from me."

It was only 7:30pm as the group filed out of the back room of *Big Jim's* and Toby was thinking about stopping at the bar and having another beer before heading home. It had been a pretty, heady evening and he needed to gear down.

As he was passing the corridor leading to the kitchen, he narrowly avoided a collision with Shirley, his waitress from a few days earlier. She was pulling her apron over her head and didn't see Toby; he caught her with both hands and steadied her to prevent a full impact.

"Hey, slow down, beautiful, I've had girls make a run for me but never had one tackle me in a public place full of people."

Shirley pulled back and immediately recognized Toby. "Well, hi handsome. Someone told me you guys were here but it's been a barn-burner tonight, and I never got a chance to stick my head in the door and say hello to Skip." Her eyes flirted playfully.

Toby flirted back. "So, you just wanted to say hi to Skip, not to me? My feelings are really hurt."

They both laughed as if they were old friends.

Shirley said, "I've got a girlfriend saving me a seat out front. We were going to have a drink, want to join us?"

Toby kept the smile. "As a matter of fact, I was just about to stop out there and have a beer before calling it a night. I'd love to."

Shirley's friend Paige was waiting with two margaritas already on the table. Toby caught a waitress and ordered one more of the tequila concoctions.

Paige was about 22, dark blonde hair that was cut short and curled down over her forehead. She was about 5'7" and slender build. Her make-up was on the heavy side, especially around her hazel eyes. Paige worked at a family restaurant a block down the street and had come as soon as her shift was over. *Big Jim's* had a small dance floor and band-stand with room for about three or four musicians in a corner right next to the table the three occupied. Shirley introduced Toby as her "cop friend" and Paige as her "food friend." The girls were in a good mood and their laughter loosened Toby until he almost forgot about the meeting in the back room.

Shirley looked at Toby seriously and asked, "So, my cop friend, what brings you out to *Big Jim's* on a week night? Were you and your friends having a serious meeting about crime or just having a beer with the boys?"

The question caught Toby for a second, but the frivolity had given Toby some confidence with the girls. "Actually it was a class on how to pick up girls on a mid-week night when the action is usually pretty slow. I must say that, so far, I'm very impressed with the results. I never thought the 'tackle the waitress coming out of the kitchen' tactic would ever work, but here we are. I'm almost speechless."

Paige was laughing so hard, she almost fell off her stool. Shirley was laughing as well but she was also looked at Toby in a way that confirmed the attraction she felt—from the first time she'd laid eyes on him. She reached her hand out to Toby. "Do you want to dance with me?"

The trio of musicians had just started a slow tune that Toby knew and he reached for her hand and led her to the small patch of boards.

Shirley slid into his arms like she'd been there before and hooked her left arm around his neck and moved with her body molded to his, never missing a step. She didn't talk, although she did occasionally leaned back against his right arm and look at him, as if trying to figure out a puzzle.

She was slow to turn him loose when the music stopped, but then smiled, "Very nice sir; not bad rhythm for a cop who's just finished his first class."

The music continued and so did the jokes and the laughter. They finished their second margarita and Paige said she was going home and offered Shirley a ride.

Shirley said, "Well in view of how dangerous this town is becoming, I thought I might call the police department and get an armed-escort home." She giggled playfully and looked pleadingly at Toby, "Do you think that they would do that for me, officer?"

Toby was totally into the mood, "I'll make the call myself and work it out."

Toby got up and walked to the back and used the men's room and when he returned, he said; "Miss, it took some string pulling but I have approval to escort you home personally."

"Yeah", shouted Shirley. "My hero has saved me, hooray!"

Toby paid for the drinks and they walked out to the Camaro, arms around each other's waists.

"Nice wheels." Shirley flirted as he held the door for her.

"My dream car, I worked and saved all through high school and college to buy her," Toby said as he put the car through her paces.

Shirley slid down in the bucket seat, "Why do guys always refer to their car as a 'her'?"

Toby, "I guess because it's so special to them. They always want it to be beautiful to look at and give them pleasure each time the go for a drive. Toby took a queue from his own words and looked carefully at Shirley. Her red hair was full bodied with tight curls over her forehead and cut just above her ears. The blond tips and occasional streaks seemed to frame her delicate face and her penetrating, hazel eyes. The short skirt revealed long, slim legs, nicely shaped hips and waist. The top two buttons of her Big Jim's shirt were opened to reveal the cleavage that held the promise of pleasure."

They arrived at her place; a small duplex in a mixed neighborhood of apartments, and modest homes. He walked around and opened her door. As she stood up from the car, she reached for him and kissed him softly and gently and he responded. Then he pulled her tight against him and hungrily explored her perfectly shaped body; her eager mouth was opened and exploring.

She pulled back and said, "You may want to lock your car? She may be here for a while and I wouldn't want anybody to steal her." Her eyes were dancing.

He locked the Camaro, and sure enough, it was hours before he came back to her. Then he drove her home and he was sure he had never heard her purr so perfectly.

CHAPTER 24

IT WAS JUST AFTER MIDNIGHT. Toby was standing next to the sign that identified a bus stop. This part of town did not justify benches for waiting commuters, as they would only be used by a homeless person as either a bed or the frame for a one room house with a cardboard roof. Therefore, Toby was leaning against the steel post that supported the sign. He was leaning against the post, rotating around it, as if he couldn't keep it straight which direction he was supposed to face, waiting for the anticipated bus.

Across the street from the bus stop was a two-story house, raised up over a basement half out of the ground. The house was desperately holding on to the remnants of a paint job that had been poorly applied about ten years ago. From the raised basement, a long flight of steps made the way up to the solid-wood, front door. Dim lighting desperately tried to penetrate the four windows, two on each level. The occupants of the dilapidated structure couldn't have tolerated any brighter light coming through their totally dilated, blood-shot eyes.

Bobby Conway was sure his eyes were ok; he squinted, to keep the bright lights from trying to blind him. There was no place to sleep here so he was ready to leave. Maybe, he thought, he would find an unlocked window to some bitch's bedroom. That would be a good place to sleep.

Nah, she would still raise hell with him after he was finished with her; he might have to kill her. Then he could have her bed with no hassle; a nice warm bed.

Bobby neared the front door, bounced off the wall on both sides, then managed to exit. He shoved the folded, white paper into his shirt pocket, careful not to spill any of the precious white powder contained inside the pocket formed by the folds.

Dammit, there's a lot of steps to this place, he thought.

At the bottom of the stairs, Bobby saw what looked like a dead animal sprawled across the bottom two steps.

Then the form moved.

No, not an animal, just a Goddamn drunk, he realized in his fog shrouded brain.

No *need to worry about him. I can jump right over him. Shit, I could jump over this fucking house if I wanted to*, he thought.

But he didn't want to jump over anything. He just wanted someplace warm to sleep.

Bobby was mumbling as he started down the steps, "Goddamn women. They keep me from sleeping. Maybe I'll go find an open window."

He saw the bus stop across the street. "I'll get a bus. There might be a woman on the bus. I'll follow her home. Yeah that's what I'll do."

Bobby staggered around the drunk and headed across the broken sidewalk.

As soon as Bobby stepped around the drunk, who had appeared passed out on the stairs, the unconscious drunk sat up alertly and flicked a Zippo lighter and touched it to a cigarette in the corner of his mouth.

Toby saw the flame from across the street. He straightened himself, turned away from the bus stop, pulled the knit hat from his head, and began walking away from the sign. A darkened Mercedes with its large engine running quietly was parked at the curb a block down the street pointing toward the bus stop.

Bobby's drug controlled senses were barely working when he reached the curb. He stepped off and began to weave across the deserted street.

The big Mercedes engine started to move the heavy car and in response to the accelerator being pushed to the floor, it leaped forward with a powerful surge of speed aimed at the figure in the middle of the street.

Bobby was suddenly aware of the intense light that invaded his sensitive eyes. The light became instantly unbearable and then a force he could not understand seemed to pick him up and slam him backward. He was faintly aware of hitting a solid wall with sharp edges. *No, it was the steps.* Then the bright light faded to blackness.

Tiny had moved fast for a big man, reaching his car in an alley around the corner from the Mercedes, about the same time he heard the impact of Bobby against the grille of the Mercedes sedan. He started his car and swung out into the street where TB was waiting. TB opened the passenger door and pulled himself into the moving car. Tiny accelerated before the passenger door was fully closed.

Fifteen minutes later, they pulled up to a concrete block building that housed a car repair business in a Ft. Worth industrial district. Timer was coming out of a side door and the Mercedes was already on a lift being cut into unrecognizable pieces.

Timer got into the back of Tiny's car as soon as it stopped and the three, sloppily-dressed men started back toward Plainfield.

*   *   *

The next morning, Toby sat in a *Starbucks* a few blocks from his apartment. Waiting for the steaming coffee to cool, he grabbed a newspaper, from a stack nearby, and began thumbing through the pages until the small story, near the bottom of the page, caught his eye.

> *"Police report a hit and run fatality in the Scanlon district of Dallas. The victim was male 35-40 years. No personal identification was found on the body. There were no witnesses, however, the medical examiner estimates the death occurred between 10:00pm and midnight. The Scanlon area is known as a drug infested part of Dallas and police suspect the man was under the influence of methamphetamines when the incident occurred. A small quantity of methamphetamines was found in the victims pockets. Anyone having information relating to this incident is asked to call 911."*

Toby sipped his coffee, and checked the sports section. The Texas Rangers had a good night against the Royals and the Cowboys started summer camp.

Looks like everyone had a good time last night, he thought, *except the serial rapist*. He finished his coffee and walked over to the waste canister. As he put the cup and napkin into the large can, he noticed a man at the counter, picking up two cups of *Starbucks*. He wasn't unusual in a way that Toby would normally notice. However, looking at the man, stirred something in Toby that kept him looking at him. Toby noticed he was glancing from left to right, giving him a 180 degree awareness of his environment. *Normal people don't check their surroundings that carefully except for armored car-couriers or diamond salesmen carrying a lot of samples.* Fortunately, Toby was behind and to the left of the man and did not fall into his range of visual radar.

Toby checked himself, broke his stare, and instinctively went back to the order-window and ordered another cup of coffee.

The clerk smiled and asked, "Was anything wrong with your first cup, or are you just getting one for the road?"

"Uh, no, I'm taking one to the office," he stammered, "for my boss."

"Lucky boss," she said with a flirting smile.

Toby stepped over by the pick-up counter and watched the man with two coffees go out the door and join another man at one of the sidewalk tables.

The first man hadn't impressed Toby with his looks, build, or any distinguishing marks. The attraction had come totally from Toby, an intuition he didn't totally understand. They had talked about this at the academy, and cautioned the young men and women to not over-react, but not ignore the curiosity that a total stranger might provoke.

The second man was different. He had a definite hardness about his eyes and mouth. His hair was jet-black, thick with jell and combed straight back. His body looked fit and muscular but his face was jowly and showed no evident benefit of Texas sunshine. He was wearing black slacks and a plain white shirt with long sleeves, fastened at the cuffs with black onyx and silver cuff-links; as the man reached for his coffee, his shirt-cuff slid up his arm just enough to reveal a tattoo just above his wrist. Toby noticed the tattoo. There was something familiar but he couldn't pull up anything specific to refer to. It looked to be snake wound around an ornate knife or dagger.

Toby picked up the new coffee and decided to sit at a table where he could observe the two men without being obvious.

The first man seemed to be explaining something to the dark companion, who occasionally interrupted with emotional expressions and gestures, leaning across the table, for confidentiality.

Toby wished for a small camera, then remembered his phone. He slipped the flat phone out of his pocket and discreetly focused on the men through the window and pushed the button on the side.

A few minutes later, the men finished their coffee and conversation and got up to leave. They didn't pick up their trash.

Toby grabbed the two empty cups and followed the pair, careful to stay at least half a block back from their furtive glances as they walked. They entered a parking lot and climbed into a black Jeep Commander and headed for the exit, another half block ahead of Toby, who hurried his pace. He got to the exit just after the Jeep came out and turned right traveling away from Toby. He could only make out the last three digits of the Texas license plate. He opened his spiral book and wrote "Tex—823."

His thoughts were conflicted as he drove to the precinct. What would he tell Perez? Would the Lieutenant think he'd recruited a fool who was trying to impress his new boss with imaginary bad guys and vague conspiracies?

He thought back to the words of the instructor at the academy. With the two coffee cups tucked in his jacket pockets, he headed back to the 3rd precinct.

*　　*　　*

"Toby, you're late! Is this how you react to a successful action, by showing up for work an hour late?"

Tip and Tyler were at their desks and were having a good chuckle at Toby's discomfort.

"I'm real sorry Lieutenant, I intended to be here early but I got delayed at *Starbucks*."

"What was her name, Romeo?" Tyler asked, and laughed.

Toby turned to Perez, lowering his voice, "Lieutenant, I may be nuts, but I noticed a couple of men at *Starbucks* that seemed odd and I just kept watching them while they had their coffee and, at times, some pretty heated conversation."

Tyler kept up the kidding, "I take back the 'Romeo.' Don't tell me we're going to have to start calling you, Bruce?"

Perez held up his hand. "OK that's it, enough of the raspberries. What else did you see, Toby?"

"After I decided to observe the men for a while, the dark-haired one reached for his coffee and I saw a tattoo above his wrist. It was a snake coiled around a knife of some kind. It seemed familiar. So I followed them to their car and tried to get their plate number."

"Did you get the number?" Perez asked, becoming more interested.

"I'm sorry, Lieutenant, I could only make out the last three digits."

Tyler got up and walked over to Toby's desk. "What, exactly, did these guys do that made you suspicious in the first place, Toby?

"I'm not sure, Tyler. It wasn't anything they did or how the first man looked. It was just something about him that made the hair stand stand-up on the back of my neck. I couldn't shake the feeling, and then when he went outside, I got a look at the other guy, who looked like he'd just as soon run over little, old ladies as help them across the street. It just seemed to confirm my first feeling. Then the tattoo just became icing on the cake. I thought I might be way out in left field but I just couldn't shake off the feeling."

Perez interrupted, "You aren't supposed to ignore your hunches, Toby. That's one of the reasons you're in this unit. You have good instincts; sometimes wrong, but usually worth checking out."

Toby suddenly reached in his jacket pocket, "That's why I took their picture and picked up their coffee cups."

Perez was shocked, "You took their picture?"

"Yeah, with my camera, I took their picture; at an angle through a window. I think it's clear enough but I'm not sure how good it'll turn out."

Perez grabbed the camera and handed it to Tip. "Get it loaded on a computer and get some help, if you need it, to tweak it for clarity. Somebody get these cups down to the lab and have them run for prints and DNA."

Ten minutes later, the four of them were crowded around a computer screen trying to match the picture with the data stored in their heads.

One by one, they shook their heads and admitted they did not recognize either of the two men. The energy seemed to drain out of the four men as they returned to their desks.

Tyler picked up his phone and said, "I'll get someone downtown on the big computer to start hunting down this partial plate. Maybe that will go somewhere."

"Toby, I want you to get on your computer and write a complete recount of everything that happened; every detail of what you saw and thought, from the time you noticed the first man until the Jeep drove off from the parking lot."

Quiet settled on the squad room as everybody found something to do with their hands, while their brains pondered the two unknown men at *Starbucks*.

*   *   *

Butch Cassidy's Steak House and Lounge was like its namesake; a maverick when it came to fine restaurants. Its steaks were second-to-none. The atmosphere was designed for the discriminating diner who wanted a choice of being seen by the right people or not being seen by anyone, all the while being cared for by a professional staff that knew how to facilitate either desire.

It was the latter that interested Ralph Wiggins and Skip Perez on this Thursday evening. Normally, the crowd was light this time of the week and the Maitre-d' had taken special care to keep his most private table, in an alcove near the back of the restaurant, available for the deputy chief of police and Lieutenant Perez. An emergency fire door was just around a large-potted, palm plant. The door was locked to arrivals but all it took was a call from Chief Wiggins to the proud boss of the dining room and the door was opened to provide the secret arrival of the two men.

The two policemen ordered drinks and said they would tell the waiter when to have the filet's put on the fire. When the drinks arrived, Wiggins raised his glass in salute and they drank from the glasses of Smirnoff Martinis.

Wiggins sat his glass down and said, "Well Skip, how's the new recruit working out?"

"Fits like a glove, so far, Ralph. It was a good idea you had to move Roberts into my squad. It seems to have put a damper on the anti-police crowd's outrage over the drugstore shooting, and so far he has impressed me and the other members of the team."

"I like it when my ideas work to the benefit of us both, Skip. You've done some very good work for the good citizens of Plainfield. Too bad we have to keep all that good work a secret but the kind of work you and your men do would be impossible to explain to the general public." Chief Wiggins seemed genuinely remorseful.

Perez waved his hand. "No regrets here, Chief, in fact we have turned the need for secrecy into a reason for pride. These boys are convinced they are leading the charge for preserving law and order, and bringing the scumbags to justice."

"You don't disagree with that conviction, do you lieutenant?" Wiggins asked.

"No sir! In fact I'm the one who suggested that idea to them in the first place." Skip Perez said with a chuckle.

They signaled the waitress to tell the chef to put the steaks on the fire and bring two more drinks.

"Any special thing I can do for you tonight?" the Chief asked.

"A couple of things, said Perez. First if any concerned inquiries come to you from the press about the hit and run in Dallas a few days ago, I suggest you just refer to the reports that it occurred in a drug infested area in another jurisdiction and from all reports you have heard about, it seems to be two drug addicts being at the same wrong place at the same time."

"I saw the item in the paper and then I learned the dead man was a very bad actor with a long sheet. I thought of you at the time, and . . . wondered?"

The steaks arrived with all the trimmings and the two began to show their appreciation.

Chief Wiggins paused after consuming half his steak and said, "Skip, you said there were two things you needed. What was the other item I can help you with?"

Skip put down his knife and fork. "I don't know if you're in the loop in any capacity with the task force on the bank robberies, but if it's possible, I would like to get a briefing on them from somebody you can trust to do that and keeping it 'between us girls.'"

"Are you trying to get dealt in that game? Why do you want that headache? They're running up one blind-alley after another, Skip," the chief said.

"Normally I'd agree and I don't want any public connection, obviously, but I may have stumbled onto a channel on this thing. My information is vague and can't be corroborated at this point and that may continue to be true. That's why my squad was formed in the first place; your original idea was for us to handle situations that could never result in an arrest or be brought to a successful prosecution. That seems to be the situation here unless my hunch is wrong."

Chief Wiggins looked worried. "You don't usually go out on a limb on hunches, Skip."

"Don't worry, Chief, I'm not going out on a limb on this either. It's just that if I know what the Task Force knows combined with what I'm sure of, it could help me confirm what I suspect."

Chief Wiggins admonished Skip to keep a short rein on any inquiry regarding the bank robbers and give a heads up before he took any definitive action. He also said, "Keep your phone on, I'll have someone call you tomorrow with a briefing."

Perez left the restaurant by the fire-exit door and started the drive home. He was mulling over the conversation he had with the deputy chief at dinner. Wiggins seemed very sensitive about Perez delving into the bank robberies. He hoped that Wiggins was not getting soft on him. Wiggins had been the one to seek him out and propose the creation of a special squad that would deal with the problems that normal law enforcement procedures were not successful in handling. The mission was a little vague to begin with; but Perez had been the right man for the job, and Wiggins was the perfect contact and go-to guy. Selected was, maybe the wrong way to describe Wiggins becoming the man to implement the formation of the group. Perez wasn't sure how many senior people in the command structure participated in the process, but during the last five years, he had developed some pretty good opinions of Wiggins as a source of information and intuition.

The squad had pulled off some remarkable maneuvers to deliver justice to men that would have escaped it otherwise. Five years of extra-legal activities could pile up on a man that wasn't prepared. Wiggins might be developing battle fatigue, he thought as he turned into his garage.

Inside, Skip went to his computer and sent a familiar message to each member of his team. "Let's get together for a burger, see you tomorrow."

Next, he called Tip's cell phone. "Tip, we need progress on that photo by burger-time. Give it your undivided attention tomorrow, OK?"

CHAPTER 25

THURSDAY MORNING, TOBY WAS WORKING on his computer at home. He had reviewed his notes on what he saw and felt at *Starbucks* four times and decided there was nothing more he could add. He hit the print button, reached for an envelope and wrote Skip's name across the flap and sealed it. He would deliver it this afternoon at *Big Jim's Burgers*. Maybe, he thought, Shirley would be there. He hadn't seen her since the night he took her home; but he'd thought about her a lot. They had really clicked like no other girl he'd ever known, and that had to be the best sex he'd ever had.

Even better than Sara, when they were at their best; before she began to fret about his job and ultimately pulled away from him feeling that the terrible hurt of separation was preferable to the devastation that might come to her door in the form of a public affairs officer; advising her of the death of Toby Roberts, killed in the service of his grateful community! No thank you. She just wasn't that strong.

His cell phone vibrated on the table next to the computer, and he was surprised to see Sonny's name on the screen.

"Hey Sonny, how the hell are you?"

"I'm still hanging in there. Trying to teach a new partner how to do police work," Sonny chuckled. "Long time, no talk, buddy; did you lose my phone number or just decide not to talk to common beat cops?"

"It's nothing like that, Sonny; things just happened so fast with Perez and once I made the move, he has had my nose to the grindstone; lots to learn. How are things with the blue uniforms? Are you writing your quota of traffic tickets?"

"Well, pretty dull, since you left; I haven't killed anybody all week." Sonny forced a laugh.

"I have to admit I've missed you, buddy; especially your sorry sense of humor. Are you still late to roll-call and sleeping through most of it?"

The good-natured ribbing helped restore the good feelings the two young officers had developed during the year they had ridden together but Toby was watching the time and soon told Sonny he needed to go in and punch the clock. They said their goodbyes and promised to get together for a beer and catch up.

When he clicked off the cell, Toby noticed a missed call from Perez. He punched the call back.

Perez was breathing hard, "Toby, I need you in the 3rd, as soon as you can get there without being pulled over. I'll fill you in when you get there."

No lunch today, he thought, and reached over to the glove box and pulled out a power bar. Ten minutes later the power bar was gone and he arrived at the precinct.

Toby climbed the stairs to the second floor and went into the squad room. Perez was in his office and Tim was sitting across from him, leaning across Skip's desk studying a sheath of paper and pictures.

Perez looked up and said; "Grab a chair TB and help us make some sense of these photos. The first picture is the one you took at Starbucks. The others were selected by the facial recognition computer. Our job is to use our professional experience and intuition and see if we agree with the computer."

"Wow, I didn't even know we had a facial recognition program," Toby mused.

"We don't but we do have friends in high places and they have an endless number of Buck Rogers's toys."

Tyler and Tiny came into the squad room and they moved the session to a conference room down the hall.

The computer program was good and had found six "probables" for the team to consider and try to narrow the choices.

Two hours later, they had a consensus on two possible suspects.

Charles Helmers had pleaded guilty to embezzlement while working as a chief teller at First State Bank in Oklahoma City. He did a plea agreement and the bank agreed to three year sentence; to avoid the publicity of a trial, which might have embarrassed other people at the bank. Helmers served 18 months at Leavenworth, in Kansas, and was released on good behavior parole, six months ago.

Six months ago, Turner Kafiq was arrested in Houston and charged with Grand Theft for a warehouse burglary, during which, a night watchman was viciously beaten. They found some of the stolen goods in his garage following an anonymous tip. Kafiq insisted he bought the items off craigslist and was nowhere near the warehouse the night of the burglary. The overworked prosecutor concluded there was insufficient evidence and dropped the charges. There was no official record of Kafiq being in DFW. Not even traffic or parking ticket.

A note in the investigators report mentioned that Kafiq's street name was "Turk".

"Where's that report from the Task Force on the bank robberies?" Skip asked.

"Here," Tyler replied, handing a file across the table to Skip.

Skip turned pages until he found the place he remembered. "Here it is. The bank teller at *Petroleum Bank and Trust* said one of the hold-up guys had an argument with another guy and he called the man "Turk." The guy called Turk called the other man, Flint. The teller said the man called Flint, seemed to be in charge. Now, we need to go back through the files and see if Flint ties in to Helmers."

By 6:00pm, the team was suffering from eye strain and stress.

Perez said, "Okay ladies, lets pack it up and move this meeting out to *Big Jim's*. We all need a break and I could eat the south end of a north bound Angus."

At Jims, the group was joined by Timer. Shirley brought beers all around. Perez was in a good mood and was kidding around as Shirley served the tall steins. When she got to Toby, she sat a long neck bottle of Lone Star in front of him and put her left hand on his right shoulder as she leaned over him.

Perez raised half out of his chair and said, "Shirley, my darling, you better be careful, before you hit my newest detective with one of your beautiful boobs and permanently cause him bodily harm." Laughter erupted around the table and Toby turned crimson down to his shirt collar.

Shirley turned to leave the room and said over her shoulder, "I think he's tough enough to handle it Skip." She flipped her butt as she went through the door.

"We have to keep our eyes on our new man, gentlemen. I bring him out here one time and he's got Shirley hot and bothered already."

Tiny joined in. "I think it may be the other way around on who's hot and bothered, Skip."

The men talked shop while they ate. They were excited over the identification of two men who were strong suspects; but at the same time, were acutely aware that there was no evidence to tie the men to the robberies; no clue to their accomplices and no idea where they might find them.

Skip was concerned about the fact that nothing in the background of the men connected to bank robbery, or DFW Metroplex, or one another. His experience taught him that there was almost always a connecting link to people's behavior and their cohorts. They just had to look further and harder.

They ordered another round of drinks and Toby got up to go to the head.

"Where you going Toby? Kiss her for me, Toby." Taunts came from the table.

Shirley met him just outside the men's room and asked, "Are you busy after you guys finish?"

"No, what time are you off?"

"In twenty minutes, I'll wait for you at the bar." She walked away, and Toby watched until she turned the corner, then he turned and walked to the back room.

There was more good natured ribbing when he re-entered the room.

Skip raised his hand. "Alright guys, I'm going to wrap this up for tonight. You did some good work today and I have good vibes but we have a way to go. First we need to get eyes on them. Each of you put out the feelers to your CIs. You have copies of TB's picture as well as mug shots from previous arrests. TB, I want you to help me on the computer tomorrow. We'll put out some inquiries to other jurisdictions but we have to be careful and not leave tracks that the Task Force might see and develop a curiosity about our interest and queer our efforts. We will have a free hand from our command but if the Task Force comes after us, the protection evaporates. OK, you know what needs to be done. Don't be bashful about communicating. You never know when—what somebody else knows—helps what you know, make sense.

They filed out of the room and everybody headed for the door, except Toby, who headed for the bar.

At first, he thought Shirley may have left, because she was not sitting at the bar. Then he looked around and saw her waving him over to a table. She stood as he got to the table and stepped to him. They merged together like old lovers and she kissed him.

She smiled warmly, and said, "Wow, now I can relax, my hero and protector is finally here."

"That's odd," Toby said, "you didn't feel relaxed. Maybe, I better check you again to be sure."

Shirley kissed him again, clinging to him longer this time. "Why have you been such a stranger officer? Don't you know a girl can be attacked and sexually assaulted in indescribable ways without having the protection she needs?"

Toby said in his official voice, "Calm down, miss, I'm sure you could describe the ways if you concentrate and take your time."

Shirley sat in one of the chairs, looking at Toby. "You're probably right, but first I want to have a drink, will you join me?"

"I thought you'd never ask," Toby said and waved a waitress over to take their order.

They continued their playful banter and sipped their drinks. Toby thought how natural he felt with this beautiful girl. She woke playfulness in him he had never discovered before. He had never been a lady's man in high school or college. He always liked them but until now, had been slightly self-conscious and unsure of what words to say, when talking to the opposite sex. It was shocking now, to hear some of the words that he spoke to Shirley without rehearsal or hesitation.

Shirley drained the last of her drink and sat the empty glass hard on the table. "That helped, I think I can do it now."

"Do what?" Toby asked

She smiled mischievously. "Give you a detailed description of the things that could be done to me. How about a ride home, officer?"

He drove the Camaro directly to her duplex and all the way, she sat as close to him as the bucket seats would allow and her hands kept him imagining what the descriptions would include when they arrived.

It was almost midnight when Shirley woke and saw Toby standing by her bed, fully dressed. "What are you doing with your clothes on, sir? Do you want me to call the police and have you arrested for decent exposure?" She stretched and yawned.

Toby resisted the urge to tear his clothes off and get back in the bed; "I've got to go babe, the Skipper wants me in the precinct first thing."

She yawned again, and said, "Oh well, the protection was great while it lasted. I hope I won't have to go so long before my next protection session. Do you think you can help me with that, officer?"

Toby was grinning. "I will make it a priority to prevent any useless delay in the deployment of your next protection detail."

She reached for him and pulled him back to the bed and insisted on giving him a final remembrance. Thirty minutes later, he had his clothes back on and resisted any further goodbye kisses.

CHAPTER 26

THE PACE REALLY PICKED UP the next morning. Cautious feelers went out, as far as the squads connections could go, but no immediate results could be claimed.

Then, about two in the afternoon, Skip got a call back from a Houston lieutenant who had shared some classes. He had visited the former girlfriend of Kafiq and she thought he was staying with a man he knew from a mutual friend who'd done time at Leavenworth. She thought the name of the guy in Dallas was Himmer . . . Hammer . . . Hummer or something like that. The former girlfriend wanted her $2,500 back that she had loaned Kafiq before he disappeared from Houston.

The weekend was half gone before they got a fix on Helmers. They were surprised when the computer spit-out an address right here in Plainfield.

Skip called out from his office, as he pulled on his jacket, "Toby, grab your camera and your notebook. We're going to take a ride and look at some real estate."

The address was located on a quiet cul-de-sac in an upper class neighborhood, and sat on a half-acre lot; heavily treed with a winding driveway leading to the 2 story house with a 3 car attached garage and an additional detached building; with two more overhead doors, one to accommodate a large motor home, alongside the driveway at right angle to the front of the house.

Skip and Toby cruised slowly, down the street, into the cul-de-sac and turned to face the big house, barely visible through the trees. Skip said, "Pretty nice set up; quiet neighborhood of professionals, who like to come home to the castle, pull up the drawbridge and live and let live. If your next-door neighbor is a mass murderer, it's okay as long as they don't get involved or have to be bothered. The lousy, real-estate market makes it easier for scumbags to rent mansions like this and nobody is the wiser. They say our real-estate has held up better than most of the country but some of the high-flyers have bit the dust and the banks have to do something to keep the money flowing, even if it was stolen from one of your brother bankers."

Skip eased his car gently back up the street, passed the curved drive, then suddenly braked to a stop. They were sitting in front of a one-story ranch set back in the middle of a cluster of Oaks. Skip was not looking at the house. He was gazing at the un-mowed grass and un-kept flower beds and shrubs.

"Write that address down, Toby; you may be about to move up in the world." Then he drove back to the precinct.

Skip made a call from a payphone to a throw away cell phone and brought Assistant Chief Wiggins up to speed on the investigation. Wiggins was cautious but finally agreed to get the use of the ranch house arranged.

Wiggins spoke in a low voice, "Perez, I want to impress on you that you are getting way out on the edge of your margins on this hunch. I have always supported your group since I authorized putting it together. So far, we have discussed your projects and given careful thought, before I have signed-off on a plan of action. This one has come out of left-field, from a rookie-cops hunch. I don't want you getting out so far ahead of me I have to *jerk your chain*. Do you follow what I'm saying?"

Perez, "Sure Chief, I'll check with you every step of the way before we make any big moves but don't worry about Roberts. He may be a little green around the edges, but his instincts are good, all cop."

Chief Wiggins, "Spare me the Blue-Line pep-talk, I wrote most of it. You don't want to start thinking you have insight into these matters far beyond my own. I assure you, you don't. Now proceed with extreme caution and keep me close."

Skip hung up the phone and stepped out of the booth. "Fucking brass, the higher up they go, the more arrogant they get."

*　　*　　*

Toby had learned that Skip was pretty laid-back when there was no pressing business. However, when the heat turned up on an investigation, he didn't know the meaning of a day off. He called Shirley and relayed the attitude of his boss to explain why he had not been in *Big Jim's* for a day or two.

Shirley said, "Well I'll have to have a talk with Perez about denying me my constitutional right to protection."

Toby, quickly, cautioned Shirley against ever talking to Skip about the operation of the squad; he would think that her and Toby were talking shop. "He wouldn't be happy with either one of us. I do want to see you as soon as I can. I will work it out, trust me; I'll talk to you soon. Bye."

When Toby got back in the precinct, Skip was in his office with a man Toby had not seen before. Tiny was at his desk, sorting the intelligence that had come in from their inquiries on Turk and Flint. He made file folders on the different scenarios the team had developed. As supporting information was developed on each scenario, it would be added to the folder until a clear picture developed or that hypothetical was totally eliminated and the folder would cease to exist.

Toby asked Tiny who the man was in the Skippers office and Tiny said he had no idea. Toby got on the phone and checked with Motor Vehicles Department to see if they had made any progress on matching the car model with the partial plate numbers. They had nothing for him.

Tiny yelled for Toby to pick up the phone. It was Andrew Garcia, President of the Texas Police Patrolmen's Association.

"Toby, you're a hard man to catch up with. How's the world treating you?"

Toby responded, "I have no complaints, Mr. Garcia, What's on your mind?"

"I talked to Russell Johnson this morning about your situation involving the shooting at Harold's Drugs a few weeks ago. Russ is going to be calling to set up a time to meet with you and get your side of the issue. We have authorized him to be your legal counsel in any proceedings that may come from the city. If you are agreeable and have no other plans for representation, then Johnson will act as your legal counsel and his fee will be covered by the association."

Toby said, "I don't have any plans, in fact I haven't heard anything lately that indicated I needed an attorney."

Garcia cleared his throat, loudly and said, "I know you have transferred to a different precinct and that may have interrupted the communication line to you but I received a call this morning, advising that the department was going to proceed with disciplinary action against you. It's standard procedure for them to advise the association, so we can prepare your defense. If it's acceptable to you, then you should follow Johnson's advice and guidance. He's had good experience in these matters and I'm sure you'll be well served. Do you have any questions for me at this time?"

Toby felt a numbness settle over his heart, "How does this work? Do I pay Johnson and get reimbursed by the association or do you pay him direct?"

Garcia said, "The association will be responsible for all the expenses generated by Mr. Johnson, Toby. His bills will come directly to the association. You will have no out of pocket expenses on this matter. I have complete confidence he will make this thing go away for you, and the association."

The stranger was leaving Perez's office and the Lieutenant waved for Toby to come in.

Perez told Toby to have a seat, then turned to the credenza behind him and picked up a file folder with a red tab. "Toby, we're going to take a big step in the bank robbery investigation. I'm going to assign you, Tyler, and Timer to close surveillance on the big house we think Turk and Flint are holed-up in. At this point, we don't know if they are the right guy's or not. Second, if they are our guy's, we don't know if the rest of the gang are staying in the house or are in some other location. As you saw, when we drove out there, the house sits on a dead-end street, in a quite neighborhood, which poses stake-out problems. We need 'eyes-on' surveillance to verify if we're on the right track. Then we can plan our strategy on how we deal with the fuckers."

Toby was processing the implications of Perez's words; "How do we get eyes-on without raising suspicion in the neighborhood, Skip?"

Perez smiled. "We become one of the neighbors, Toby my man. I have arranged for us to quietly have use of the ranch, back in the grove of trees. I'll give all three of you guys more details tomorrow at 9:00am, here in my office."

It was near lunch time so Toby decided to drive over to *Big Idea Burgers* where his kid brother worked and catch up with the family gossip. Toby had stayed close to Todd as his brother went through the tough transition through his teen years, which was tough enough on any kid. Then the drugs had thrown him completely. For three or four years his personality had changed and he had rejected any authority or respect for normal rules of behavior from his family or legal authorities. However, this past year he seemed to be getting back his moral compass and showed signs of returning to the Todd his family knew and loved. For the last eight months he had held the job at *Big Idea Burgers*, waiting tables and serving gourmet hamburgers to the upscale clientele. He had not missed a day and Toby wanted to give him all the moral support he could so he made an effort to come in and have a burger every couple of weeks.

Todd was just coming from the kitchen with a tray of burgers and Mexican fries, when he saw Toby coming through the entrance. He told the table captain, to find Toby a seat at one of his tables and went off to deliver his cargo.

Toby had made his selection when Todd came to his table. He stood and put his arms around his brother and gave him a strong hug, then held him back and looked him over carefully. "God, you're gaining weight! Is it the burgers or the cooking your getting at home?"

Todd smiled broadly. "It's just good clean living brother, you should try it."

"I keep promising myself to do that but my bad habits keep overpowering my good intentions. How the hell are you and that beautiful girlfriend doing?" Toby asked as he sat back down.

Todd beamed. "We are getting along just great. She's way too good to me but as long as she keeps her grade point above 3.0, I guess I'll put up with her."

Toby slapped him playfully on the shoulder and said, "You better do more than put up with her, little brother. You know she's the best thing that's happened to you in a very long time."

"I can confirm that, big brother. How's Karen treating you?"

"When I see her, she treats me fine. We haven't been able to get together much lately." Toby was searching for a way to change the subject.

"What's going on Toby, are you two having trouble?"

"No Todd, not trouble. We just seem to be on different wave lengths these days."

"Whose wave length are you on, big brother?"

Toby hesitated, and then said, "I did meet someone recently. She's a lot of fun and I find myself thinking about her more during the day and wishing I was with her more often. She's very different from Karen; but I still have good feelings for Karen."

Todd picked up Toby's burger and when he sat it front of Toby, he asked, "Which head are you using, when you're thinking about this new girl?"

Toby blushed, "I have to admit the sex is fantastic. The best I've ever had, but it's more than that. We are totally comfortable with each other. We crack jokes and laugh at each other without offending the other. I know it's totally unlike me but it just happened. I'm not jumping out of the plane yet but at the same time, I'm trying on parachutes."

Todd saw his brother was serious. He put his hand on Toby's shoulder and said, "Well I'm not going to rain on your parade, big brother. You've always been the one with common-sense and sharp instincts so don't doubt yourself too much on this. You may have stumbled onto something good for you. I will be happy for you if you have."

Toby finished his burger and gave Todd a hug. "I appreciate you, little brother. You have come a long way in a very short time, don't slow down, and give Cindy my love."

Toby climbed into the Camaro and headed towards Shirley's duplex.

Shirley opened the door wearing red halter-top, blue shorts and a white scarf tied around her neck. For a moment he could only stare and appreciate her freshness.

Finally he spoke, "Wow, if you were on a flag-pole, I'd salute you and sing "The Stars Spangled Banner."

"Well, if you'll come in out of the heat, you can supply your own pole and salute me all you want. But, forget the singing; I'll put on some music."

She pulled him in and shut the door. Then she wrapped herself around him with every part of her body touching him in all the right places and kissed him with her full, giving lips telling him how glad she was to see him.

An hour later, she pulled carefully away from him and announced she had to clean up and get to work.

Toby decided to join her in the shower where they washed each other and then toweled each other dry. It was arguably the best shower Toby had ever had. He dressed and kissed her on the neck as he told her goodbye. "I'm going to be pretty much out of circulation for the next few days but I'll call you when I have the right opportunity."

Shirley turned and smiled. "OK, and by the way, you need to work on your salute. Your form is perfect but I bet you could hold it longer with more practice."

She was still giggling as he went out the door.

*　　*　　*

The next morning, Tyler, Timer, and Toby were seated in Perez's office. Perez spoke, "Here's the story guy's. You will go to the grocery this afternoon and get enough food and toilet stuff for two or three days. There's a bag of supplies there in the corner; A spotting scope and tri-pod, three night vision goggles, an ultra sensitive remote microphone that transmits up to a thousand feet and an infrared camera that can record a fly at a hundred feet and record him taking a crap. Pick up a voice recorder downstairs." The group looked at each other and grinned.

Perez continued, "The plan is to get close enough to the house to determine how many people are inside. A specific count is very important. Next, as many pictures as you can take without spooking them will help ID the occupants. Third and last, get as much recording as possible to find out what their planning and bragging about their past deeds."

Timer interrupted, "Skip, what about some contact mics if we can get up to the windows?"

"Good thinking, I forgot to mention them, there are six of them in the bag. I think that about covers it, guys, is there any more questions? If not, I'm sure you don't need to be reminded that if they figure out we're looking at them, we'll blow the whole job and they'll run like rabbits. Right now they think their operating with total anonymity. Let's keep the element of surprise on our side, OK?"

Tyler volunteered to do the grocery shopping and Toby and Timer went home to grab a couple of clothes changes and a shave bag. Tyler came and picked the other two up about eleven. They wanted the neighborhood asleep when they arrived and unloaded the supplies.

Tyler was driving a black Ford van from the motor pool, with the brake lights wired to a disable switch. He killed the lights and flipped the switch as he turned onto the cul-de-sac and moved carefully and silently to the drive leading to the low, one story house in the cluster of Oak's. Toby pushed the button on the remote opener Perez had supplied and one of the garage doors began to open. The Ford slid into the garage and Toby pushed again to close the door before the car had stopped moving. They hurriedly carried their gear in and put the food in the two door fridge which was working, thanks to Perez.

They went through the house with a roll if black vinyl, cutting it to size and taping it in place on each window.

They decided to use three, battery-powered lanterns to avoid making too much light and to keep the light directed to the floor, not the ceiling. The waited until about one o'clock before they killed all the lights and donned the infrared night goggles.

Out the back door, they could clearly see the sprawling back yards of the luxury homes along this side of the street. True to Texas suburban standards, there were no fences; just a generous scattering of shrubs and trees that almost guaranteed protected movement as they went from house to house to their target.

The big Tudor house was totally dark and Timer intuitively went to three windows across the back and attached a contact microphone to each.

When he re-joined the other two, he said, "I think I got two bedrooms and the kitchen. I'm going around the other side and get one on the living room. I don't think they have anyone on guard duty. They're sleeping like babies in their cribs."

While Timer went around the large house, Toby and Tyler placed a radio microphone in a bush near the back porch, tapping it securely to a sturdy limb. Timer returned and the three went back to set up their listening post.

"How many microphones did you put up, Timer?" Asked Tyler

"Two more when I went around the house, for a total of five, and I have one left if we need it; but I think we may have the down stairs covered."

"Well, it's 3:00am," said Tyler, "I suggest we roll out the sleeping bags and take a nap. The receiver will be our alarm. When they start moving around, I'll wake up."

Toby asked, "How are going to wake up without an alarm?"

Tyler smiled as he said, "I did this kind of stuff in Iraq, during the first skirmish. I carry my alarm clock in my head. If I tell myself to be alert for unusual noise, a mouse running across the floor will have me wide awake. If you don't hear them, I'll nudge you."

*   *   *

Toby was having a dream. Karen was shaking her finger and scolding him fiercely on one side and Shirley was lying in her bed holding the blanket open for him to join her. He was frozen, unable to move in any direction. He was struggling so hard to move, he was shaking. Then the shaking grew harder and he found himself looking up into the coal black eyes of Tyler.

"Come on TB, it's time to earn your pay"

Voices were coming over the receiver clear enough to be understood but nothing important yet; a lot of cursing, farting and complaining about having to fix breakfast

The three listeners fixed themselves some cold cereal and settled into, what might be, a boring day. It took a while to start compartmentalizing the voices. They had the receiver plugged into a recorder and a voice-recognition scanner showing the voice pattern variations on a paper tape. Not state of the art; but a reference to compare with, as more voices were recorded.

More variations soon appeared and the team became increasingly optimistic that they had the whole gang inside the big house. At one point, a few were horsing around and an outburst came loud and clear. "Turk, you stupid bastard, you didn't turn the stove off when you finished. Are you trying to burn the fucking place down, or what?"

Then a different voice, "Just shut you're fucking mouth Flint; you're like a little old lady. Get off my fucking back."

High fives went back and forth between the three investigators. Tyler punched his phone and speed dialed Perez.

Before long the gang was heard debating over how long they were going to be holed-up in the house before they went after another bank. One suggested they should go to another area, pull a couple of jobs to make the police think they had given up on DFW, then come back and hit them again, when they weren't looking. That got a big round of laughs.

Flint's voice said, "Everybody needs to cool their jets. We'll get the word when it's time to do another job and we'll be told what job and where. The first two were text book so let's not be changing the game plan. If we stay cool and do our job, we'll be ready to retire before you know it."

The thought weighed on Toby, who were they waiting for and what action would Perez make, now that they had the group cornered. None of what they now knew could be used to make an arrest. A judge would throw the case out of court and probably throw the TTs in jail for its illegal conduct. Would Perez order the execution of the whole bunch; like the rapist they had run down in the dark street? This would be a massacre. He felt a shiver go through him and turned his attention back to the receiver.

The rest of the day was uneventful; idle talk through the day and then that evening, after dinner, four or five members of the gang had gone out on the large back deck for cigars and brandy. Their conversation wasn't clearly detectable through the contact mics and the directional microphone was scratchy; listeners could make out some references to the bank robberies. One remark was directed to Turk, regarding the death of the teller in the second robbery.

"That maniac is the one that shot both tellers," Timer spit out the words.

There was more chatter about moving to a new area until DFW cooled down. Kansas City, Oklahoma City and Houston were the most mentioned. The men continued the drinking until most just seemed to drop out of the conversation one by one until the house became quite.

The team discussed the option of going back up to the house and trying to get some pictures that could be used for identification, but finally decided the benefits did not justify the risks of discovery.

They called Perez and brought him into the picture and detailed the caution they were exercising. Perez agreed that exposure of the surveillance would be disastrous. Perez told them to sleep in shifts in case developments should accelerate, and he would talk to them tomorrow.

The next morning, Perez called and told the team to continue the recordings and monitor any movements of anyone leaving the house.

About two in the afternoon, someone complained about running low on liquor and two of them, Toke and Paca, were appointed to go to the liquor store in the nearby shopping center and were to come right back. "No screwing around now," Flint warned the two; as they went out to the garage.

The team alerted Perez and he called the liquor store manager and asked him to put the money aside that the two used for their purchase, and he would send Tiny over to change money so they could check the serial numbers against the bank lists.

The liquor buyers were back in forty-five minutes and the sound of bottles came through loud and clear as they were unpacked.

Perez called about five o'clock and reported positive matches on the bills from the liquor store. He said he was coming out to join them just after dark.

It was 8:30 when Perez opened the middle garage door and joined the team. Tiny and Tip followed him from the garage.

Tyler spoke, "Wow, we've got the whole team; gonna be a big night, Skip?"

"Could be, Tyler; depends on our friends down the street. If they party tonight like last night, I think we may join the party." Perez said with a wink.

The party got underway. The confinement was weighing on the group and they had a fresh supply of frustration relievers. They went through the normal phases. First they got loud and boastful about their conquests. Second they got angry with each other, the system, their parole officers, and police. Then, they just got angry. They finally quieted down about midnight and the mics began to pick up the sounds of drunken sleep.

Perez went out to the garage and came back with a bulging gym bag. He sat it on the table and invited the men to help themselves. He said the guns inside were totally clean; all Mac 10s with extra clips and silencers. He divided the officers into four teams; two men each—in Team 1 and 2; one man each—in Team 3 and 4. Team 1, was to go in the front door and clear the living room, hall and front parlor, Team 2 was to go in the back door, clearing the kitchen, two back bedrooms and bath. Teams 3 and 4 would climb the two trees on the north and south sides of the house to the edge of the roof that extended beneath the windows of two of the three upstairs bedrooms.

Perez tapped the floor plans he'd brought with him and then handed each man a pair of latex gloves. "I expect most of them to be passed-out on the first floor on couches or in chairs. The two men upstairs should finish quickly and move on downstairs, but don't get sloppy and miss one of them. Now, put on your gloves, and then make sure your silencers are on tight and your weapon is ready to fire in short bursts. This is not a discussion club. We are here to rid our community of this little bunch of malignant tumors. So just think of yourselves as professional surgeons. Let's get it done!"

Perez started to get his Mac from the bag, then turned and said, "We'll go over across the back yards and when we arrive at target, we'll give the upstairs boys a count of thirty to get in their positions. I'll give the signal to go—on the walkie-talkies. Good luck to us all."

Toby was on the back door which, he discovered, had not been locked. As Perez gave the signal, the sound of a shattered window pierced the stillness. Toby and Tip pushed through the kitchen door just as one of the targets started walking toward the foot of the stairs to check out the sound of broken glass. He sensed the back door had opened. He turned, a Glock with the hammer back in the cocked position in his right hand. Toby pulled hard on the trigger under his right forefinger and the gun barely moved as four deadly missiles left the machine and formed a straight line across the man's chest.

While Toby stared at the fallen bank robber, Tip rushed past Toby and entered the bedroom on his left. Toby heard the half cry of what—and then the soft thump, thump, thump, thump; Then no sound at all.

It was over in five minutes.

Perez told them to leave the victims where they fell and he hurried to plant physical evidence that would suggest the shooting was a fight between gangs and that these interlopers were the recipients of street justice. When he had finished, Perez came down the stairs carrying a large duffel bag in each hand. "Alright guys, leave the Mac's and clean up everything else. I want this place to look like we were never here; just the dead scum and some other scum, bad guys, who came to kill the competition, and deliver a message."

The next hour was spent removing the contacts and other equipment that might be a clue to other police investigators of their presence. Then they loaded the remaining supplies and equipment from the single story house and drove away with all lights off until they reached the end of the cul-de-sac.

*   *   *

Toby walked through the large vacant room and entered a wide hall. There were no doors on either side, just a seemingly, endless row of walls on each side of him. He had to get out of the hall but he knew he could not turn back. He had to keep moving forward. The hall turned to the right and then quickly back to the left, then he was in darkness, but he could see light just ahead. He kept moving forward. When he turned the next corner, he saw two doors, one on his left and one on the right. The doors were wide and he could see clearly, everything in each room beyond the doors.

In the room on the left was a large bed and a sofa piled with cushions. Karen was sitting on the sofa looking back at him and she seemed to be staring at his hands. Toby looked down and saw his hands were drenched with blood. Karen looked back to his eyes with sadness and a trace of fear.

The room on the right was identical to the other but there was no one sitting on the sofa. Shirley was in the bed, with a playful, yet loving look in her eyes. She smiled knowingly and seemed to be calling his name. She reached out to him with one hand while the other hand pulled back the satin sheet and exposed her perfectly formed, naked body. She held the sheet higher and beckoned him to come through the door and join her.

Toby felt frozen in place; unable to move in either direction. When he looked back at Karen, he seemed to see his Mom and Dad faintly, in the background.

Then he looked at Shirley and felt such a longing for her playful way of loving him; enjoying him, he ached, and broke into a sweat.

Toby bolted upright in his bed and looked around to make sure he was in his apartment. He got out of bed, pulled on some jeans and went to the kitchen and punched the coffee maker. Soon, he was working on his first cup of the strong, black stimulant and began to feel better. It was four o'clock in the afternoon and he still felt a sleep hangover that would have allowed him to go back to bed and return to sleep and to the dream. He went to the bathroom and turned the shower on hot and stayed in it for a long time.

After the shower and a close shave, Toby checked his phone and saw he'd missed three calls. He checked his messages. They were from Shirley, his mother, and Russell Johnson; the attorney for the TPPA advising him of a hearing before the Police Review Board in two days.

He called Johnson and set an appointment for one o'clock tomorrow afternoon to review the issues that would be addressed at the hearing on Wednesday at 10:00am.

Shirley had left for her shift at *Big Jim's*, so he called his mother. She said Dad was on the road and wouldn't return till Friday. She complained that she hadn't seen him for so long and he told her he would be out in a half hour if she would fix him a sandwich and a glass of milk. He grabbed a light jacket and jumped in the Camaro. He pulled onto the I-30 freeway and opened up the Camaro for about eight miles. That cleared some carbon out of the powerful engine and some cobwebs out of his head. He arrived at his mother's quicker than his estimate.

They had a good visit. Toby had always been able to talk to his mom, but today he found himself more guarded about what subjects he opened. Then she opened the subject that was on both of their minds.

"I haven't seen or heard from Karen for a while; how's she doing?" His mom asked, trying to sound casual.

Toby, also trying to be casual, said, "I think she's doing fine Mom. We haven't gotten together much lately. Between her schedule and mine it's been difficult, but I have talked to her on the phone. I called her last week when I had a day off, but she had already made plans with some of her girlfriends, for a girl's night out and my schedule has been pretty tight since."

His mom puttered at the kitchen counter, "Well, you don't work day and night, it seems like you two could figure out a little personal time together."

Toby finished his glass of milk and handed her the glass. "Don't worry mom, Karen has to work it out in her mind, if she can deal with my job. I think that's part of the reason we don't get together as often as we would if she was at ease with that issue. By the way, Mom, I went over and had a burger the other day at *Big Idea Burgers* and let your youngest son feed me lunch; have you seen him lately?"

"Yes, he comes by every few days. I see more of him than you." she pouted.

Toby left his mom knowing he felt good about spending an hour with her and thought his visit had reassured her and cheered her up. He felt good anytime he lifted his mom's spirits.

Toby pointed the Camaro toward *Big Jim's* and pushed down firmly on the gas pedal.

Shirley was surprised to see Toby walk into the saloon. She led him back toward the kitchen and kissed him on the mouth.

"I can see reports of your death were greatly exaggerated but you are looking a little sickly, can I get you something to eat? I'm going to be a couple of hours before I get off. Can you stay?" Shirley said, playing with his shirt buttons.

"I'm all yours for the evening and I'm hungry." Toby replied with a smile.

Shirley squeezed his arm as she turned him toward the bar area. Looking back at him as they walked, she said, "You're hard to train, mister, but I'm happy to report you're making real progress."

Toby laughed and watched her exciting walk, as he followed her to a table.

He finished a beer and a burger and ordered bourbon and seven while he waited for Shirley's shift to end. When she was finished, she came to his table, pulled one of the empty chairs over to his and sat as close to him as she could. She leaned over and whispered in his ear, "It's almost illegal how much I've missed you. If you hadn't warned me off, I would have called Perez to see if you had been shot."

Toby looked into her beautiful green eyes and said, "I know how you feel, but I'm as serious as a heart attack when I tell you that you mustn't ever do that. When I can, I'll come to you. When I can't, there's nothing you can do about it. Do you understand?"

Shirley said, "Wow that was a mouthful. Take me home, so I can properly show you how much I appreciate that promise."

Toby was hers for the evening and the rest of the night. He wasn't sure how many times they woke and re-affirmed their passion and fell back to sleep holding each other as if they feared turning loose might be forever.

He woke at 8:00 and Shirley was not in the bed. Then he caught the aroma of bacon and coffee. For a second, he thought he caught a gas smell, but the aroma from the bacon distracted his concern. He got in her shower and let the water beat on him and put him in a good mood, with his appetite surging.

Shirley greeted him with a kiss as she carried two plates to the table.

Toby said mockingly, "She cook's too?"

She retorted, "Listen mister, I'll not have you running around town telling all your friends that I'm just a sex toy. I don't deny the claim, but I'm a lot more and it's time you realized it." She twisted her butt as she passed him, giggling.

He was finishing his eggs when he remembered. "Hey, before I got in the shower, I thought I smelled gas; did you notice that?"

"Yes, when I first came into the kitchen," she answered. "I checked the stove and found the line was a little loose at the wall connection."

Toby was concerned, "Why didn't you call me, what did you do?"

"I got a crescent wrench and tightened the connection," she said.

Toby smiled up at her, "Damn, she can cook and do house repairs, too."

He finished breakfast and headed for his appointment. The smell of gas lingered in his thoughts.

*   *   *

Russell Johnson's law office was in a three-story stucco clad building. His office occupied the south-west corner and the sun was making the three room suite bright and straining the air conditioning units against the sweltering heat that persisted in continuing the three years of drought that had plagued the state.

The secretary/receptionist was a slight built blond with a short straight hair cut that barely covered her ears. She wore pink and white-framed glasses and a two-piece suit with the same colors. She announced Toby into the phone and Johnson promptly came to the door and welcomed him. The lawyer's private office was spacious and he offered Toby a seat at a 6'X4', mahogany table to one side of the room.

Johnson began, "Toby, I want to thank you for coming in this afternoon. This is an opportunity for us to get comfortable with each other and for you to fill in any gaps I may have missed after reviewing the police reports on the three incidents that the review board will be referring to in tomorrow's hearing. The primary focus will be on the shooting of Eddy Sandusky when he was driving away from Harold's Drug Store at 607 Tarrant, in the early morning hours of May 12th. The Internal Affairs Department has recommended that you be found guilty of violating Department Regulation R-251. Their position is that you had received training on all the regulations and were fully aware of the prohibition on deadly force when a suspect was fleeing the scene of a crime."

Toby, feeling the anger rise in him, asked," Mister Johnson, have you read the transcript of my interview with IAD where that question was raised?"

"Yes, Toby, I have and I'm glad you raise that question. Why don't you go ahead and tell me your interpretation of R-251?"

Toby leaned forward, and began, "I understood that if I was approaching the scene of a reported crime and saw someone running away from the scene, I would be prohibited from making an assumption about, number one; the identity, and number two; concluding the person fleeing was responsible for the reported crime. In fact under that scenario, I wouldn't even know for sure if a crime had been committed until I investigated the report or the alarm. Under that scenario, regulation R-251 would forbid the use of deadly force."

Johnson sat back in his chair and twirled his pencil. Then the attorney asked, "How, then, do you justify your shooting on the occasion in question?"

Toby answered immediately, "I was under attack from a man using deadly force, and I know department rules allow me to use deadly force in reaction to deadly force."

Johnson smiled and made some notes. "You're exactly right, Toby, its regulation R-252 that spells out that specific authority. Do you think you can give the Review Board that same statement tomorrow?"

Toby replied, "I'm sure I can. It's pretty much what I told IAD and the top brass, but they don't seem to listen. I don't get it."

Johnson closed the file folder. "Toby, I have to be honest with you; this is a societal problem and you have taken the lid off the boiling pot. For many years now, there has been a growing discontent with police, rigid rules, and guns. The peace-nicks have been getting better organized and gaining influence at all levels of society, and with most of our politicians. I'm satisfied you made a clean shoot, but I'm concerned about our ability to persuade the board to go against the thinking of some pretty influential groups in this community. The politicians are mostly running for cover with their tails between their legs. I don't want to discourage you but I want you to be realistic. You just tell the board, tomorrow, what you told me today, and I'll do the rest. The association is solidly behind you and I'll do my best to get them to listen to reason."

Toby went down to the Camero, and called Ron Perry. "Hi Ron, it's Toby Roberts, how are you?"

Perry said, "I'm just fine, Toby, but from the scuttlebutt, you're not doing so well. What can I do for you?"

"I don't know Ron. You're probably the most solid police officer I know. I need to talk to someone I respect and trust and your name came up at the top of the list."

"If there's anything I can do, Toby, I guarantee I'm there for you. I've told you before; you're one of the best rookies I've ever started. From all I've heard, you did a clean shoot and the brass knows it, but next year there's an election for Mayor and half the city council. That's where your problem comes from, politics."

"I don't know what I can do to fight City Hall, do you, Ron?"

"Remember what I told you Toby; there's a big difference between what you know, and what they think. You have to demonstrate to everyone that your justification in the shooting was exactly correct and any objective judge would not find otherwise. I understand you've got an attorney from the association. Use him for all he's worth and follow his advice. If he thinks I can be helpful, have him call me and I'll talk to him. Good luck buddy."

Toby drove to his apartment and called Sonny Montgomery. "Sonny, its Toby. Yes, I'm OK, I'm getting ready to go before the review board tomorrow, and I was wondering if they had called you as a witness or anything?"

"They haven't, Toby, and I've been expecting to hear from them anytime. We both shot at the Pontiac and yet, I've been questioned one time, and that was right after the shooting. I don't know why they're crucifying you and not even talking to me. If you need me, I'll be glad to come down as a corroborating witness."

"I'll let you know Sonny, but I don't want to screw up your career in the department for no good purpose. I'll let you know how it goes, so long pal."

Toby changed into shorts and a tank-top, opened a beer, and started a recorded episode of Blue Bloods and started bringing his blood pressure down before going to bed.

*　　*　　*

The next morning, Toby woke fresh and optimistic about the hearing. He walked out to the row of yellow boxes and pulled his copy of the morning paper. It was not yet seven o'clock and still pretty quiet in the apartment complex. As he turned back to his opened door, he noticed a car parked at an odd angle. It wasn't in one of the marked slots reserved for the tenants. *If the manager catches that before you leave, he'll have a fit*, thought Toby.

He took a few more steps toward the opened door when he saw something move out of the corner of his eye. There was a man sitting behind the wheel of the car.

The car was a newer model BMW. He hadn't seen the driver at first. Had the man been lying down in the seat, or reaching down for something he'd dropped?

There has to be bucket seats, Toby thought. Not a good place to lie down. The windows were tinted against the Texas sun and Toby could not get a good look at the man.

The BMWs engine came to life and the car quickly began to back up.

Toby had changed directions now, walking toward the car. He was, suddenly, conscious of the fact he was not armed and approaching an unusual vehicle under suspicious circumstances. He stopped.

The BMW had backed into the main driveway. The driver had cranked the wheel hard to the left then back to the right while throwing the shift down and the tires squealed as the car sped out of the parking area and onto the street.

Toby stood still for a few seconds, replaying the scene that had just occurred. He finally shrugged it off and went in to read his paper and prepare for his big day.

CHAPTER 27

I T WAS 9:20AM AND THE hearing was underway. There hadn't been any bomb shells from the board and Johnson's strategy for Toby was to keep the emotions on a leash and try to focus the minds of the inquisitors on **the legal difference between running from a crime scene and attacking a police officer while resisting arrest.**

The lawyer for the Board was speaking, "Officer Roberts, you seem to have had a series of pretty violent episodes in recent months. Did you have an image of yourself as a shoot-em-up, Dodge City kind of cop when you joined the Plainfield Police Department?"

"No sir, in fact I saw my role in the purist's definition of the Protect and Serve motto that we all subscribe to. I gave up an opportunity for a very exciting life, playing college and probably professional soccer. I had a couple of exciting years in high school and had a full ride scholarship at a top university, so I had a picture of what might be ahead for me. I turned away from that for four years of small college, with no scholarship, studying criminal behavior and investigation techniques. Then when I graduated, Plainfield had no openings, so I flipped burgers for two years waiting for an opportunity."

The chairman interrupted, "Officer Roberts, I'm curious about your claim that you reacted to an attack from the suspect as opposed to shooting the man because he wouldn't stop when you ordered him to. Did that argument originate with your attorney, Mister Johnson?"

Toby said, "No sir that explanation is the truth and I told that to Mr. Johnson the first time we met."

The Chairman continued, "So, the question is, do you fancy yourself a lawyer, who can interpret the law and department regulations as you perform your patrol duties? Are you a lawyer or a policeman?"

Toby felt Johnsons hand on his arm, cautioning him to not get into an argument with the chairman.

Toby gathered himself and spoke, "Sir, I just consider myself a fortunate police officer, whose had the benefit of a good education and some excellent training by my department. I understand, this is a legal proceeding we are in here today and my attorney may not approve, but do I have the board's permission to speak candidly?"

The chairman looked across the face of each member. "Of course, Officer Roberts, you're free to say whatever you like."

Toby ignored the look of alarm on Johnsons face. He stood and began to speak in a moderate, reflective voice; "I've been a police officer now for almost two years. For Two years before coming on the Plainfield force, I flipped hamburgers and served coffee, waiting for a vacancy. For the four years prior to that, I attended college and earned a degree in criminal justice and law enforcement. During this time I was convinced I would use all the training and education in a total commitment to my community and my profession and honor the oath I took when I joined the department."

Johnson was on his feet. "If it pleases the board, I object to you allowing this testimony without my previous approval of its content."

The board members huddled and the chairman spoke, "Mr. Johnson, your client asked for our permission to say what's on his mind. We will allow him to continue if he chooses or stop now. It's up to him. Officer Roberts, what is your pleasure?"

Toby avoided looking at Johnson and said, "Mr. Chairman, I have said most of what I have to say and I would like to finish."

The chairman saw nods of approval and said, "Then you may continue."

Toby's face was set with apparent calm, "In spite of my formal education and excellent training from Plainfield Police Department, there was a crucial element I did not learn until the events that are responsible for our gathering here today, took place. All the training in the world cannot prepare a police officer for the critical few moments when he confronts someone in the act of committing a crime and commands them to stop and submit themselves to the authority of the enforcer of the law.

I have given much thought to the mental process that occurs in the mind of a police officer under threat of a hostile act that could end his life or the life of someone he's trying to protect. It's a thought that keeps going through my head since I have found myself in that situation more than once in a very short period of time. My conclusion is that an officer has a very short time period to assess the situation in light of what he sees and what information he's been given. My estimate is a maximum of two minutes to assess the situation before he takes action, and then about 10 seconds to act correctly or face the possibility of death to him or others he's trying to protect.

"Your ruling on this matter is very important to me and my future as a policeman. However, I don't think the effect you're ruling may have will end with this hearing. Thank you for your attention."

Toby paused as if he might continue then, sat down.

A murmur went through the crowd of onlookers

The Chairman declared the hearing in recess until further notice being sent to the respondent and his attorney, and adjourned in time for a late lunch.

Johnson told Toby if he ever wanted to give up police work, he might consider law school. He said he should go on with his duties and he would call him when he heard from the Board Attorney.

Toby got in the Camaro and headed for the 3rd. A couple of times, he thought he saw a black BMW two or three cars back, but each time he changed lanes to get a better look, it wasn't there. He drove on to work.

Perez pulled into the massive parking lot in front of the home of The Dallas Cowboys. The lot seemed big enough on any game day, but when there were only two cars present, it had a dwarfing effect on the visitors. A Crown Victoria entered the lot and stopped next to Perez. The driver was a heavily built man, a scar above his left eye that ran almost to his ear. He was in his late 40's or more, built bulkily but looked agile as he got out from behind the wheel and came to the rear of Perez's car. Perez opened the trunk and removed two duffel bags and carried them to the Crown Vic, placing them in the larger trunk.

The windows were totally blacked out, making it impossible to see any other occupants. Without a word, the driver got back in the Ford and drove out of the lot.

"Your welcome," Perez said to the empty parking lot, "any time you want a half million dollars delivered, just call me and say when and where." He got back in his Pontiac and drove to the 3rd.

It was almost 3:00 in the afternoon by the time the five members of the squad drifted into the office. Perez was the last to arrive and after he checked his desk, he said; "Ok guy's, I don't want to keep you long so let's go in the conference room for a few words. I'll get you out quick."

In the conference room, Perez got right down to business. "OK, I want to start by telling you what a good job you did. A CIA Special Ops unit wouldn't have done any better. I don't want any chatter about the exercise, ever coming back to me. None, never! If you were expecting more than a pat on the back from me, just be patient. Everything that goes around comes around. There were knowing looks around the table and every man knew that they wouldn't be chatting about the episode around the office.

After the meeting, Toby walked to his desk and had decided to stay a while and clean up some paper work and read some NCIC chatter on the computer, when he heard the girl at the front desk. "Toby, pick up line 2, it's Southwest Hospital."

Toby felt a cold chill coarse through his body, as he heard the officious voice deliver the terrible news.

*   *   *

Toby raced down the flight of stairs, pushing the door button on the remote, as he raced to the Camaro. He slapped the auxiliary red flasher on the roof and screeched out of the parking lot, horn blowing all the way.

He arrived at the huge medical complex in record time and swerved the Camaro into the ambulance entrance in the rear of the hospital. He flashed his badge at a security guard at the sliding door and handed him the Camaro keys. Put the car in a slot that won't be a problem and point me to emergency surgery!" He said to the guard.

Down the corridor, he stopped a nurse and explained who he was and who he was looking for. She pointed him down another corridor to Surgery #4. He ran to the door of #4 but was told he had to wait in the small area of plastic chairs, and someone would talk to him as soon as they knew the status of Ms. Blaylock.

Toby wasn't sure he felt so strongly for Shirley, until he heard the officious voice on the phone, asking if he was related to Shirley Blaylock. He explained their relationship, and then they advised him that Shirley Blaylock had been transported to their emergency with extensive injuries following a hit and run accident. They said his business card from the Plainfield Police Department was found in her wallet and no other identification except Shirley's driver's license and social security card.

He got a cup of coffee at the courtesy stand in the waiting area and paced in the corridor until a doctor came out of surgery and asked, "Are you Toby Roberts?"

Toby answered in a tentative voice, "Yes I am. How is she, doctor?"

The doctor locked his hands behind his back, "She's stable and we will move her shortly to recovery where we can keep a close watch for a while. Your business card was found in her purse and little more except driver's license and social security. Do you mind telling me what your relationship is with Ms. Blaylock?"

Toby said, "We're very good friends, doctor, and if there's anything she needs, please tell me."

"Does she have any family we can talk to?" The doctor asked.

"None local, I know of, when can I talk to her? Toby fidgeted.

"An hour or so, she is stabilizing pretty fast and she is strong and appears in good health."

"Can you tell me what her injuries are?" Toby asked.

"Outwardly, just minor cuts, mostly from hitting the blacktop street. We had to remove some pieces of the rock from her head and around her left ear. She'll have a couple of bald spots around the injuries which will grow back quickly. It could have been far worse but we were able to tuck the wounds back together and the scarring should be minimal. Her main issue is internal damage, resulting from the impact from the car. However she's lucky that she has only one broken bone and that is the lower rib on the right side. I would guess that's where the car struck her.

All things considered, she's a pretty lucky girl. We'll know better as we observe her and run test's and scans over the next day or two. Right now I'm thinking it's mostly bruises which should heal with plenty of rest." The doctor said he would make another evaluation tonight before he left the hospital.

Toby waited an hour and forty minutes before a nurse came out and said he could see Shirley for five minutes, as they had given her a sedative and she would be getting sleepy pretty soon.

His heart dropped to his stomach, when he approached her bed and saw the bruises around her eyes and the heavy bandages on her neck and around her head. He hesitated a moment, then leaned over and kissed her on the cheek.

She opened her heavy eyes and whispered, "I'll give you an hour to stop that, mister."

Toby's heart soared back to normal and beyond. "Behave, yourself, lady." I leave you alone for a day and look what happens. Does it hurt, bad?"

Shirley opened her eyes and whispered, "Not as bad as it did when they first brought me here. That was really bad. They've got good drug's here. Promise you won't raid the place."

She smiled and then started to cough. A nurse came in and said Toby should leave because the talking would aggravate the coughing.

"Shirley, did you see the car? Can you remember anything?" Toby asked as he stood to leave.

"Small, low, I think a sports car; black?" Shirley closed her eyes as the drug began to deliver its promised relief.

Toby kissed her cheek again, and reluctantly left the room.

At the nurse's station, a uniformed cop was getting information he needed to complete his report. He spotted Toby and came over, cutting him off from the sliding doors.

"Hear you're on the force; a relative?"

"I'm Toby Roberts, 3rd precinct, and you're?"

"Sanders; Rod Sanders. Traffic Patrol, out of headquarters. I didn't catch your relation to the injured girl."

Toby thought about leaving the patrolman standing, and walking through the sliding door. He needed to get someplace and digest all the events of the last few days. There were too many things, out of the ordinary, for him to be comfortable with. "I didn't say, but I am a very close friend, and I will appreciate it if I can stay in touch with you so you can keep me apprised of any progress on identifying the car or driver, okay?"

The patrolman pulled a card from his pocket. "Sure thing, anything to cooperate with a brother in blue. She wasn't very helpful; too groggy to say very much, but I'll come back tomorrow when, hopefully, she'll feel better and clearer."

Toby left the hospital feeling like a swarm of hornets were hovering around his back, each one trying to decide where to plant his stinger, and then let the others have what was left.

He drove the Camaro randomly until he had an idea. Who could help him sort things into lists. If he could categorize the events into what, when, how, and why maybe he could get a handle on who!

Toby pulled his phone and punched in Ron Perry. Perry answered, "Hi Toby, what can I do for you?"

Toby said, "How about meeting me in 30 minutes at *Big Idea Burgers* and let me buy you a burger and a beer."

Ron said, "How did you know I hadn't eaten?"

Toby gassed up the Camaro and was at *Big Idea Burgers* in twenty minutes. He told Todd he needed privacy, two Burger Meal Specials, and two long necks.

Ron Perry was late and the burgers arrived the same time he did.

Sorry I'm late Toby but Assistant Chief Wiggins wanted to bend my ear just as I was headed for the door. What's up anyway? Our conversation a day or two ago was pretty brief; is there something new?"

Toby told Perry to go ahead and start on his burger. "Like I told you before, Ron, there's no one in the department I would trust or respect the judgment of, more than yourself. I have had a pretty wild bunch of things happen to me and people close to me in a very short period of time and it's starting to scare me a little. Most of the fear comes from not knowing why or who could be wanting to do me harm. The usual riffraff I can handle, but today, it occurred to me that it's not the street that's causing my problems and I don't have the experience to know who else it could be."

"Calm down, Toby, eat some of your burger and have some beer. I'm in no hurry," Ron Perry said, as he took a pull on his beer.

"To begin with, there are some activities I can't tell you about because I have been sworn to secrecy. I can tell you I'm okay with what I've done and I don't see how that could be causing the series of events that concern me."

Perry held up one hand and said, "Toby, I understand that there are certain elements of police work that have to be kept confidential and even though you're still relatively new at it, I'll assume you're right about the activities. Now, just tell me what happened."

"Okay Ron, here goes. A few days ago, I spent the night with my girlfriend. She got up before me in the morning, and went to the kitchen to fix some breakfast."

"Sounds like my kind of woman." Perry smiled.

Toby continued, "When I got up and went to take a shower I thought I could smell gas, but the bacon aroma was strong and I put it out of my mind. Later, Shirley said she smelled gas when she first went to the kitchen. She found the gas connection to the stove was loose so she tightened it and went on with breakfast. When I left for the precinct, I saw a black BMW improperly parked in her parking lot. As I approached the car to tell the man he should move, he started the BMW and squealed out to the street.

Toby flushed a little then continued, "Then, yesterday, I had to go before the Police Review Board, on the drug store shooting. I thought there was an unreasonable prejudice against me from them but, as you had advised, I wrote it off to political correctness run amok, and shrugged it off. After I left the hearing, I kept seeing a black BMW darting in and out of traffic behind me. After a while I didn't see it anymore, so I just decided I was imagining something that wasn't there, and I went on to the precinct. This afternoon, I had a meeting at the 3rd and when I came out I got a call from the hospital that my girlfriend had been brought in, the victim of a hit and run."

"My God, Toby, I'm so sorry, is she going to be alright?" Ron Perry asked.

"I think so. The doctor said it'd take a day or two before he knows about the internal injuries. Right now, she looks worse because of the cuts, scrapes and bruises, but just before I left, I asked if she saw the car or remembered anything about it."

"Did she remember anything, Toby?" Perry asked

"All she said was it was a sports-car, black, low. I immediately recalled the BMW and I have to admit a chill went up my back."

Ron Perry chewed the last morsel of his burger, and washed it down with a big swallow of the beer. "Toby, I understand about the activities you can't tell me about and I'm not going to pry. You've had more than your share of conflict on the job, recently. Has anyone talked to you by phone or in person in a critical or angry manner about any of the incidents where you used force against the people you were apprehending? Any threats from anyone or phone calls where the caller just hung up without saying anything?"

Toby shook his head. "No Ron I'm pretty sure I would remember someone doing things like that, and I don't.

Ron continued, "Maybe your girlfriend has an ex that's not happy about you spending the night in the bed that used to be his. Has she talked about former male acquaintances?"

Toby said, "To be honest, no. Neither one of us has talked about our past love lives, but I don't think she has been involved with anyone seriously enough to provoke revenge. I have the feeling that all this might be directed at me, and if she can be the instrument of getting at me, then it must be because of something I've done. The part that stumps me is who it could be? What have I done to anyone?"

"Toby," exclaimed Ron, "you have shot one man twice, shot and killed another, and stuck a gun so far into a fat mans belly, he probably shit his pants. Now, I think it's reasonable to assume that someone could be pretty unhappy with you."

They talked for about forty-five minutes and Toby's thoughts did become clearer but at the end, he still had no suspects, if there were any. Toby drove the Camaro to his apartment and went to the front door.

There was a plain envelope stuck in his door. He took it in and tore it open. The paper was plain, with no discernible marks except the simple typed words, *YOU DON'T HAVE TO GET HURT-JUST*

FOLLOW DIRECTIONS AND KNOCK OFF THE HEROICS! YOU HAVE BEEN WARNED.

Toby's hands shook as he carefully put the paper back into the envelope and laid it on the kitchen table. He would take it into the lab tomorrow and have it checked for prints and any DNA.

He took a long, hot, shower which did drain some of the tension from his body and went to bed. His thoughts were on Shirley and how sad it had made him to see her battered and cut body and hurting inside.

He slept, fitfully, while flashes of images of a black car bearing down on Shirley as she stood in a wide street but she seemed unable to move. Toby was there, watching in horror, as the car drew closer, Toby strained to reach and pull Shirley to safety, but he couldn't move a muscle. Then the car was within inches of hitting her, Toby could make out the driver bent over the wheel, his heavy shoulders bent forward, making his expensively tailored suit stretch unnaturally. His position behind the steering wheel was poised with a look of authority, and his thick black hair framed his face which was pure white, with no features.

Toby awoke with an involuntary jerk and his eyes were wide open. He thought about the blank face, and rationalized that there was no reason he could put a face to the figure in the car. The note had confirmed his suspicions that someone was unhappy with him and if harming Shirley delivered the message to him clearly and definitively, then, they had no hesitation to use that method.

He finally slept and didn't even hear the radio when the alarm turned it on and then off, an hour later. He was sweaty when he woke, so he showered off again, then went into the kitchen and fixed a bowl of cold cereal. The phone rang and he grabbed it before the second ring.

"Roberts, this is assistant Chief Wiggins. How are you doing these days?"

Toby was caught off guard. "I'm fine Chief, getting around a little late. I was just about to go out the door. What can I do for you this morning?"

"I would like you to swing by headquarters, on your way to the 3rd. We need to have a little chat, OK?"

When Toby left his apartment and walked to the Camaro, he glanced down the row of cars parked in their assigned spaces their trunks forming a logical pattern of shapes and angles and tail light configurations that only computers would come up with. Then the headlights interrupted the pattern and jumped out at him. They were small and perfectly round and built into the only car that was parked by backing-in instead of nose first. It was black and he could make out a familiar emblem centered in the front of the hood. The black letters, BMW, were clearly visible across the blue emblem. He climbed in the Camaro, and instead of going left, out of the parking area, he went right and did a 360 degree around and as he drove slowly, he looked carefully at the BMW, which appeared to be empty. He scanned the apartment buildings and parked cars but didn't detect any people or shadows that seemed out of place. He drove out onto the street feeling the presence of the black BMW following behind.

It was 9:30 AM when Toby pulled in behind police headquarters. He took the stairs up to the second floor and entered Chief Wiggin's office.

The girl, at the desk, announced him to Wiggins and the usual ten minutes went by before the chief told the receptionist to send him in.

Wiggins didn't stand or offer to shake hands. He just waved Toby to an empty chair and continued to peruse a paper to which he put his signature, and buzzed the girl to come in and get it in the mail.

"Roberts, I thought it was time you and I had a catch-up visit. I try to do this as often as I can with newer officers. I may have been negligent with you. It appears you have been getting into one sticky situation after another." The chief said, and looked directly at Toby.

"Yes sir, I guess you could say lady luck has been looking the other way when I'm on duty." Toby squirmed.

The chief came back, "I fail to see the humor in your files, which I have right here on my desk."

"Yes sir, I didn't mean to be flippant about my experience on the job. I have taken my job very seriously since I joined the PPD." Toby squirmed more.

Chief Wiggins held up his right hand with forefinger extended. "Maybe, too seriously, Officer Roberts. Many new officers make the mistake of trying too hard to change the world in their first two years on the job. Policemen have to learn how the world works. Then, with experience and know how; they can have a positive effect on the part of the world they're responsible for. Do you follow me, Officer Roberts?"

Toby nodded his head. "Yes sir, I think so."

Wiggins went on, "There are ways for a smart, talented officer to get ahead. The most important way, is to let his senior officers lead. Good senior officers need and appreciate young recruits who make good followers. If you pay close attention and follow a few basic rules, you'll advance up the ranks and know firsthand what I'm talking about. Are you happy in your current assignment, Roberts?"

"Yes sir, I am. I get along with the other men and think Lieutenant Perez is a good leader."

The chief smiled broadly, "Then slow down, young man, and let him lead. You'll find things go a lot smoother all the way around. Now, I've got a barn-burner day ahead of me, but I'm glad we took these few minutes. Communications are what keep the world turning, Roberts. Thanks for coming by."

The receptionist barely looked up as he walked out of the office and headed downstairs.

Back at The 3rd, only Tiny and Timer were in the squad room. Toby grabbed the phone and called the hospital to get an update on Shirley. The head nurse said she'd gotten a good night's sleep and all the vitals were stable. So far, so good.

The local papers were full of information about the mysterious shooting at the big house in the up-scale neighborhood. Neighbors said they hadn't seen any of the men well enough to recognize any of them. In fact, some neighbors didn't know any one was living there while others just thought it was a couple who liked their privacy and was keeping to themselves. Two geniuses promoted the theory that it had to be a falling out among thieves and if these were the bank robbers, the killers must have made off with the money.

Toby wondered about the money; there had to have been five to six hundred thousand dollars left when the TT squad conducted the attack. He was rationalizing the killings, but the thought of Perez stealing the money was over the top. He could not justify the police robbing the robbers of money that belonged to the banks. People had been killed and wounded over that money and it was the job of the police to bring justice and apply it to the criminals who committed the crime. He could not be at peace, thinking about himself as a common thief.

Toby's cell phone vibrated against his hip and he punched the answer button. "Roberts here, how can I help you?"

"Officer Roberts, this is Calvin Rodgers. I'm the president and manager of International Bureau of Investigation. I believe you have met my wife Emily. She told me about her CCPS organization giving you and your partner an award about a month ago for some pretty brave conduct on your part."

Toby replied, "That's very kind of you sir, and very much appreciated. Your wife was a very generous and gracious lady and my partner and I were pretty overwhelmed with the honor. What can I do for you today?"

"I may be sticking my nose in where it doesn't fit, but my wife is very sure you're an honest cop with a sense of honor. Not something you find every day. I wonder if you could break away and meet me for lunch tomorrow?"

"I don't see any problem with that, can we make it about 11:30am? That'll get us in ahead of the crowd. I'll only have an hour or so. Where do you want to meet?"

"Come to the *Olive Garden* near the Mall, and ask for Cal Rodgers, I'll already be at a table." Rodgers hung up.

Things were pretty dead around the squad room all day. Perez never did show or call. It was around 4:00 in the afternoon when Toby decided to pack it in, saying he had some personal stuff to do and he headed for the Hospital.

Shirley was awake when he walked into her room. Her eyes opened wider and she grinned as she said, "Thank God, my protection detail finally arrived."

Toby leaned over her bed and kissed her gently on her un-damaged cheek, and said, "There was a sign downstairs that said a dancing girl was putting on a show in this room, so I came right up. Has the show started yet?"

Her grin spread. "The show was postponed, due to technical difficulties. Hang around, though, I'm giving rain checks for a future performance."

"On a more serious note, the head nurse says you have been behaving yourself today and are doing far better than they thought you could last night."

She smiled at the words. "Pessimist's, that's what they are around here, pessimists. I told them I'm going home in two days and they will learn I'm a woman of my word. How's the world treating you without me to keep an eye on you?"

"I'm good. Things are pretty quite at the precinct. I think all the criminals took some time off this week, so I can concentrate on getting you well and back home."

Shirley laughed and then groaned from the pain inside.

Toby rose out of his chair. "I'm sorry. Okay, no more jokes. Does it hurt pretty badly?"

"It's better today. They say some parts came loose in there and are going to hurt while they grow back. When that happens, I'll be better than ever, so you should be going to the gym for a while, so you can handle the treatment I'm giving you later." She grimaced with pain again and Toby saw her push the button on the pain killer pump.

Within a minute, she began to drift off into the dream world that was free from pain and her eyes closed.

The nurse came in and checked her vitals and said, "The morphine will keep her out for a while. She has been asking for you every time she wakes up today. I've got your phone number at the station and I promise to call if anything important happens."

Toby asked, "Has anyone else been in to see her or made inquiries by phone since she was brought in?"

"No, no one." The nurse said, "At least, not since I came on at two o'clock."

"Can you see her door from your desk at the nurses' station?" Toby asked.

"Yes, but I have eight patients I'm keeping track of, so I'm not looking at her door all the time. Why, are you concerned about someone coming to see her that shouldn't be in there with her? I know she was a hit and run victim. Do you think someone wants to hurt her?"

Toby said, "I just want her watched very carefully. If I need to have a police officer here, I will arrange it, so just alert your relief to keep a close eye on her and give me a call if anything unusual occurs."

Toby left the hospital and drove the Camaro home, taking his time and making two stops. The second stop was at a Mobil station for gas and it caught the guy in the car behind him off guard, and he had to drive the BMW passed the station and circle the block. Toby was watching as he came back around a corner and pulled to the curb about a half block down from the station, killed the lights. Toby could see, by the exhaust that the driver had kept the car running while he waited.

When Toby was finished filling the gas tank, he eased out of the station and watched in the rear view mirror as the BMW maintained a half block between it and the Camaro. There were no threatening moves from the Beamer so when Toby reached his apartment, he parked and walked normally into his apartment.

I'd rather have you watching me tonight, you son of a bitch, than bothering Shirley at the hospital, he thought to himself.

He went to bed about 10:00pm and slept relatively sound; no dreams with girls shaking their fingers or inviting him to their bed.

The next morning, he could see the black car across the street and fifty yards down. The driver was slumped down in the front like he had slept in that position.

Good for you, motherfucker, I hope your neck is so sore; you can't turn your head. He called the squad and caught Perez. He told him about Shirley, and Perez said he should take the day on personal time and stay with her. When he hung up, he called his old precinct and caught Sonny on his way to his car. "Sonny, I've got a black BMW giving me a problem; sticking to my tail like we're connected by a tow-bar. About 11:00am, it's important I go somewhere without company. You think you could light him up for me and run him off long enough for me to disappear?"

Sonny enthusiastically replied, "Hell yes, Toby. I'll ticket him for loitering if you want."

"My guess is that he will rabbit on you as soon as he sees your lights and hears the squawk. Just play it careful and run him off. Thanks a lot partner, I owe you."

Toby called the hospital and was told that Shirley had a good night. She had eaten some breakfast and was napping. He breathed easier and got ready to leave.

At 11:00am sharp, a black and white cruiser turned onto Toby's street, three blocks back from his apartment. Sonny turned on his red, white, and blue light bar across the roof. The BMW motor started instantly, and drove hurriedly down the street. It turned at the first corner and disappeared. Toby was in the Camaro quickly and left for his appointment.

Toby pulled into the large parking lot at *Olive Garden* and parked near the front entrance. Inside, he asked for Cal Rogers and was escorted to a booth in the back of the restaurant. The man in the booth was wearing a black suit with a white crew-neck, knit shirt. His black hair receded halfway back on each side leaving a peninsula of black hair extending to his forehead and combed straight back. The thin black moustache, perfectly trimmed, completed the look of a character right out of a Mickey Spillane Movie. He slid out of the booth, exposing his 6'2" height generous stomach and freshly shined Italian wingtips.

"Cal Rodgers, at your service, Officer Roberts; thanks for coming down."

Toby reached for the handshake. "Toby Roberts, Cal, pleased to meet you and, I appreciate the invitation to lunch." Toby said as they both sat down across from each other in the booth.

The waiter came and they got their orders, pasta and the house salad for Toby and soup and salad for Rogers, in ahead of the crowd.

When the waiter left the table, Toby looked over at Rodgers and said, "Like I said Cal, I appreciate it but I have to admit I'm not sure why I'm here, having lunch with the top private detective in the Metroplex. I'm not looking for a job change, if that's what you have in mind."

Cal Roberts put both hands flat on the table, and said, "Toby, my wife is a very good judge of people, and when she came home after giving you and your partner their award, she said you were an unusually dedicated young policeman and that's what her group was looking for in our community. When my wife is that impressed, I make a mental note and file it away for future reference; and I did just that.

Then, a couple of days ago, I was visiting with one of my most knowledgeable CIs, and he told me about some unusual information regarding the laundering of some serious amounts of cash. My man plays both sides of the street the law lives on, and he says some bad actors are getting set up to convert some dirty US dollars to a clean commodity, bring that commodity back into the port of Galveston and sell it for clean dollars or at least dollars that would be difficult to trace. Normally I would have ignored that kind of gossip. It happens every day somewhere along the gulf coast. However my man mentioned the name of a company based in Ft. Worth, that I am very familiar with."

Toby swallowed some fettuccini and asked, "I don't see how this story relates to me?"

Rodgers continued, "Maybe it doesn't, but you may be able to connect information you have in the police department with what I'm telling you, and the connection may come together. I'm still relying on my wife's intuition, you understand?"

Toby nodded, "Maybe. Please go on."

Rodgers looked directly at Toby, "I'm putting a lot of trust in my wife's opinion of people, she's never failed me before, but I want you to appreciate the fact that I've got a feeling about this. A bad feeling, and when I decided that the police needed to know what my man had told me, I didn't know any police officer I could trust, totally, to take this to it's just conclusion. My line of work has taught me that corruption is wide-spread through police departments everywhere but in spite of that, they're thousands of hard working, honest cops who are motivated by the ideal of protecting the helpless and serving the greater population with a relatively peaceful community where justice can be delivered to everyone. I've had dealings involving this company before, and I can tell you, it's a shell, operated by one man for the sole purpose of generating clean money to increase his, already sizable income."

Toby was trying to get his head around the implications of this information. He held up his hand, Mr. Rodgers I'm impressed by your opinion of my character, and I hope it's well placed, but I don't see how I have the experience or the ability to intervene in something that could be a lot bigger than I am."

"Toby, you are absolutely right. You'll have to have help, and there may be ways I can get involved. We have to see what you can put together with what I have. Then, if some sort of action is needed, I have the connections and experience to help you in ways you haven't thought of. Is what I've told you so far making any bells ring? Do you have knowledge of anything that connects with what I've told you?"

Toby's mind raced. Could he trust this man or could he be part of the group behind the events of the last few days. How could he confide in someone who claims to know about a mysterious man, probably prominent to some degree, and influential? Then, again, how could he not confide in someone with more capabilities and connections and know how than he had?

Toby made a decision, "Mr. Rodgers, I think I'm going to have to rely on your wife in the same way you did when you decided to approach me. At the same time, I have to move very cautiously and make sure I don't put myself in jeopardy. If you trust me at this point enough to give me the name of the company you mentioned, I will pull information together and we will meet again in a couple of days. I tell you this, I cannot move ahead with any of this unless I have your full assistance with all the assets you claim to have at your disposal."

Cal Rodgers signed the charge slip and put his credit card back in his wallet and smiled. "Toby, I have to remember to tell my wife, when I get home tonight, that she's still the smartest woman I know. By the way, the name of that company is Gulf Trading Partners, SA. And it's located in Ft. Worth's industrial area. I look forward to our next meeting!"

It was 1:30pm and Toby was glad he'd called and gotten Perez's OK for PT. At the same time, he wondered if he'd told the wrong man about Shirley. Did Perez already know? Toby knew he'd taken the bank robbery money from the house after the shooting. It would be hard for Perez to make that much money, just disappear. So, where did he take it? Who did he give it to? He didn't turn it in. He couldn't have. That sum of money would call attention to itself, no matter what steps were taken to conceal it. At the same time, Toby thought, it would take some very skillful maneuvers and well thought out stories to arrange the discovery and recovery of the stolen money and protect the anonymity of the TT's.

He pulled the Camaro into the parking lot of the hospital and looked for a parking slot. He'd just spotted one, when he noticed that just three parking slots further down—was the nose of the black BMW pointing out toward the driveway. *Didn't this idiot know, by now, that that parking technique made him stand out like a sore, thumb?*

Toby parked the Camaro and walked over to the BMW. The man was lying back in the seat, pretending sleep. Toby tapped on the window, and the man lowered it half way, "Yeah, what do you want?"

Toby drew his Glock, cocked it as he pushed it through the opened window, and pushed the barrel into the hollow of the man's neck, just under his jaw. "I'll tell you what I want and what I don't want motherfucker. When I look out my apartment window, or drive down the street, or come to the hospital to see my girlfriend, I don't want to see this BMW or any other car with you behind the wheel anywhere in my sight. What I do want is to see your absence any and everywhere I look. If I do see you again, I'll shoot you and take that gun you have in your pocket and put it in your dead hand and pull the trigger. You'll be just another scumbag who tried, unsuccessfully, to kill a cop."

Toby pulled the gun back out the window and said, "Now, get the fuck out of my sight before I change my mind and just shoot your sorry ass right here and now."

The man's hands were shaking but fury was shooting out of his eyes, as he turned the key and squealed the tires out of the lot and onto the street.

Toby had stopped his own shaking by the time he got up to Shirley's room. They had moved her from intensive care, to a regular room on the second floor. When he walked up to her room, he saw Sonny sitting in a chair outside her door. Toby gave Sonny a bear-hug and said, "Man, you don't know what it does to me to see you sitting out here. I feel guilty enough, thinking that this happened to her because of me."

Sonny clapped him on the shoulder and said, "Don't worry about it, partner; I'm glad to help. I'm not sure what's going on but all you need to do is yell and I'll be wherever you need me and help any way I can."

"I may be yelling quicker than you think. Things are bunching up on me and my situation might get very sticky. You may want to think twice before being dealt a hand in this game. No hard feelings if you pass on it."

Sonny shrugged and said, "You can transfer a dozen times and you'll still be my partner. You taught me some good stuff when I started, and you were a good model for me. I'll be there for you if you need me. I'm going to take off now. Call me later."

I'm one lucky guy, thought Toby, as he watched Sonny walk to the elevator and disappear.

He went into the room and was thrilled to see Shirley's bed in a raised position and her sipping on a glass of juice.

"Hey, you better let me check the contents of that glass for alcohol. There are rules in this hospital and as a sworn officer of the law; I have to make sure you're in compliance."

Shirley laughed and sat the glass on her tray. "Come over here, Officer Roberts, I have something that needs to be investigated by the police. It's very urgent!" She flashed a mischievous smile.

He crossed quickly to the bed, and looked down at her with stern eyes and a furrowed brow. In an official voice, he asked, "Now what seems to be the specific problem, Miss?

"There's an area just below my nose that feels almost numb. I thought someone was going to come by and treat the problem but no one showed up until you walked in. Do you think you can help me?"

"Yes", Toby said, "If you'll shut up." He leaned down and kissed her firmly on the mouth. A little too firmly, he thought, as he felt her flinch.

Toby stepped back and said, "Sorry, did I hurt you?"

Shirley looked at him thoughtfully, and said, "Yes you did, and I'm thinking about filing a complaint. Not for kissing me too hard, but for neglecting me for twenty four hours then sending a substitute as a replacement. The very idea, thinking you could be replaced;

total bad judgment on your part. Maybe I'll make that part of my complaint."

He sat in a chair by her bed, "You really are feeling better aren't you. So feisty, I may have them increase you dosage of knock out drops."

She settled back into the thin pillow and said, "Seriously, I love you for sending Sonny over to sit outside my door. I was able to get three hours of the best sleep I've had in a few days. It was very sweet."

Toby moved to sit on the edge of the bed and said, "It was more than sweet. I don't want to make you worry but I think it's important you know; I have suspicions that you were hit deliberately, and it's probably my fault, not yours. So you can expect to see more policemen drooling around your door until I can get you out of here." The nurse came in and said it was time for a nap. Toby kissed her and went out to the hall and sat in the chair by the door.

He pulled out his cell phone and called his dad. "Dad, this is Toby, where are you?

Darren Roberts answered. "Houston, for the next two days, what can I do for you Toby?"

"I need some information on a company with offices in Galveston and a warehouse in Ft. Worth. Do you have time to do some checking for me?"

"I'll take the time! What kind of information are you looking for?" Darren Roberts asked.

"I want the owner or owners, where it's headquartered, what it does to make money, when it started, and any names of principals or employees involved in the company's business activities." Toby said.

Darren Roberts asked, "You also want to know where its corporate headquarters are located?"

"Yes, I'm sorry; this is a little new to me."

"What's the name of this mysterious business, Toby?"

"Gulf Trading Partners, SA," Toby said. "And I don't know what the SA stands for."

"I'll get everything available and call you tomorrow before noon."

"Dad, I want this over my cell phone and if I don't answer when you call, I'll call you right back, OK?"

The shift changed at 2:00pm and the nurse from yesterday remembered him and the comments he had made to her regarding Shirley's security. She visited a while and said, "If you want to stay here tonight, you can sleep in the other bed in her room. It's unoccupied now and no one is scheduled for it at this time. You're going to be exhausted if you try to sleep in that chair."

Shirley was thrilled that he was spending the night and it took till 9:00 that night and a healthy shot of morphine to get her settled down and off to sleep."

Toby finally drifted off, into a dream world populated by cops shooting a lot of people but when the shooting stopped, bad guys in black were still standing.

He woke with a start, and saw a woman in a long white coat standing over Shirley. "What are you doing there?" Toby asked.

The woman jumped and spun around, revealing dark clothing under the white coat. The woman's hair moved in an un-natural manner, and Toby's hand reached under his pillow for his gun. The figure bolted toward the door, nurse's cap and the hair it was pinned to falling to the floor, as the woman, who now appeared to be a man, ran from the room, and out into the deserted hall. Toby heard something hit the tile floor as the fleeing figure, raced toward the stairs and plunge through the door. Toby looked down and saw the hypodermic needle lying just outside the door. He resisted the urge to pick it up and, instead, ran back into the room to Shirley. He grabbed the signal cord and pushed the call button. The nurse was in the room in seconds.

"What happened here," the nurse commanded.

"I woke up and saw someone who looked like you, bent over her. I asked what she was doing and she turned and ran from the room, dropping that hypodermic on the way out. The wig on the floor suggests the intruder was actually a man" Toby said.

The nurse bent to pick up the syringe as Toby yelled, "Don't touch that, I'll get a cloth to pick it up. Can you get me a sealable bag to put it in? There may be prints."

A doctor, who'd just come in to make his rounds came in the room and checked Shirley over. She was fine, although a little groggy and confused about the abrupt interruption of her drug assisted sleep.

It was 5:10am and the nurses were ready to begin the morning routine. Toby had a few minutes to explain to Shirley what had stirred both of them from their sleep. She was scared but Toby's presence was reassuring and he went out into the hall so the nurses could perform their morning routine.

Toby called Sonny and woke him up. "Sonny, we just had an episode here at the hospital. Shirley's OK but it was a good thing I was here. I was hoping you could swing by and stay till roll-call when I can relieve you. I'm going to see if I can get her out of here today."

Shirley was happy when she knew Sonny was going to stay but not very pleased that Toby was leaving. He told her he was going to try and get the doctor to discharge her today and he was working on a place to take her later this afternoon.

He drove the Camaro to The 3rd and parked in the lot. There was no BMW in his rear view mirror on the way.

CHAPTER 28

TOBY HAD TO DO A lot of explaining to his mother when he called and asked if he could bring a lady friend to her house to stay a few days, and that a strange man would be parked outside, to make sure no one bothered her or his friend during the day, and that he would be sleeping there for the next few nights.

Toby then called his dad and filled him in on the proposed house guest. "Dad, I know this is a real imposition on you and Mom and if you don't like the plan, I'll understand.

Darren Roberts thought for, what seemed like a long time, and then said, "I am concerned about your Mom's safety and peace of mind. However if she made no objection and doesn't call me in the next few minutes and veto the idea, we'll go with the plan. I am reassured that Sonny will be there to keep an eye on her. Consider it's a go unless you hear different from me.

Darren Roberts then gave Toby the report on Gulf Trading Partners, SA . . .

Darrin Roberts reported, "The Company is registered in Panama, obviously to take advantage of the tax code or lack of it down there, as well as loose banking laws. It's hard to get the corporate officers, but Walter Forsythe, Dallas, Texas, is listed as Legal Counsel and agent. I'm e-mailing the report, which includes addresses of the business in Panama, Galveston, and Ft. Worth."

"The name Forsythe is familiar to me," Toby said.

"Should be, he's legal counsel for the Citizens Advisory Board for the Plainfield Police Department, and a board member for The United Fund." Darrin Roberts informed his son. "Can you tell me what you're into, Toby? This stuff gives me a bad feeling and now you're hiding a friend out at our house. I don't want to hesitate to do whatever you need from me and Mom, and I guess you'll tell us what's going on, when you think you can."

Toby said, "You're terrific Dad. No matter what comes up, you and Mom are always there for me." Toby clicked off the call.

Toby referenced his cell's directory and called Cal Rodgers. "Cal? Toby Roberts. Things are moving faster than I anticipated. I need some help. Can you meet me near Southwestern Hospital? I'm going to get Shirley out of there today. Someone tried to get to her last night. Thankfully, I was staying in her room and ran the guy off. I'll tell you everything I know when I meet you. Where and when can you meet me?"

"Toby, there's a little coffee shop one block north of the ambulance entrance. It has a garden area with outdoor dining tables. We'll have privacy there. See you in thirty minutes.

Toby caught the doctor at the nurse's station and after vigorous debate, persuaded him that Shirley would be safer out of the hospital. The doctor said she would be ready to leave about 4:00pm. Toby said goodbye to Shirley. Sonny said he had to be at roll-call by 5:00pm and Toby assured him he would be back by 3:00.

Cindy's Garden was a quiet, peaceful place for nurses and doctors to escape the stress of their jobs and enjoy simple foods and beverages served with efficient awareness of the urgent need for speed. The outdoor dining was set like a garden with lattice partitions covered by different vines sporting blossoms of red, pink and white.

Calvin Rodgers was waiting in one of the secluded nooks in the outdoor dining area.

Toby took a chair and pulled the report out of an expansion file case he'd appropriated from the nurse's station.

"You'll see in the report that an attorney named Walter Forsythe is the attorney for the company Gulf Trading Partners, SA. I suspect he's the whole company. It's registered in Panama, and has addresses in Galveston and Ft. Worth. The report lists 'import-export' as their type of business.

Cal interjected, "That's what half the illegal-operators in the gulf-coast, states claim as their business."

Toby continued, "Cal, based on what you told me earlier, I need to tell you some very confidential information about an operation inside the Plainfield PD. The unit conducting this operation is off the radar and I have sworn not to discuss their activities. I must confess it's, **'our'** not **'their'** activities. I'm a member of the group I'm telling you about. As you may have read or heard, the review board is giving me a rough time over the shooting at *Ralph's Drugs*. Lieutenant Perez approached me about joining a special squad that he commands. He said I wouldn't be harassed by the politician police anymore and I'd be judged by my results, not by technical department rules. It sounded good, so I transferred to his command about two months ago. It's been a busy two months and I'm starting to have some misgivings about the work we're doing. I'm going to trust you to keep this information between us, until I clear you to share it with anyone else. Are you OK with these conditions?"

Rodgers looked at Toby for a long time, then spoke, "Toby, my wife is an even better judge of people than I suspected. I agree that we are partners in this operation, and as long as we're both able to make rational decisions, I'll wait for your signal to talk to anyone else. If, in the event, you should be killed or disabled, I reserve the right to use my own judgment on how to use what I know."

Toby spent the next thirty minutes filling Roberts in on the activities that had led Toby to this meeting, including his concern about Perez and his involvement in the big picture.

Cal Rodgers talked as if he was thinking out loud. "Perez may not be culpable in the big picture. The six-hundred grand is the big unknown. Why did Perez take the money, when he knew everybody on the squad saw him carry the two duffels out of the house in plain view of all of you? I have to assume someone told him to remove the money and it would be worked into the public version of apprehending the gang by someone at a higher pay grade than Perez. The thing I can't figure is—who he may have given it too. I'm not sure I see him directly connected to Forsythe. He's not in Forsythe's league and guys like Forsythe like to have lots of layers between themselves and the people who get their hands dirty."

Toby, also thinking out loud, said, "But Cal, no apprehension or capture occurred. The police have picked up on, and ran with, the speculative story in the press that a rival gang came in and after the shootout, simply took the money. I remember that Perez seemed to concoct that story while we were still at the scene of the shooting."

Cal sneered. "Yeah, and that's a very convenient story that, in my thinking, is too good for a newspaper reporter to have conveniently made up. I'll bet my own money, that story was planted with the reporter, giving someone the opportunity to agree with the theory."

Toby said, "And that someone would have strong ties with the reporter that originally put out the theory; someone with considerable influence in PPD."

Cal Rodgers was drumming his fingers on the table. "Toby, I don't think it's a good idea to take Shirley to your parent's home. If we're on the right track, then we're dealing with people who're both ruthless and have the power to twist facts; and make the ones they can't twist, simply go away. I do work for some very large and powerful companies, and from time to time, they have visitors in town, that they do not want registered in one of the fine hotels in the area. Part of my responsibilities to my clients is to provide a safe house for their comfort and private transportation until they leave. You should not put your parents in harm's way. We have to assume your personnel records are easily available to these people and they wouldn't hesitate to go to your folk's house any more than to the hospital last night. You go to the hospital and get Shirley. When you're ready to leave with her, call my cell and I'll give you directions."

*   *   *

They had waited until 5:00PM to take Shirley out of her room. When Toby called Cal to give him the time table, Cal told him his plan for removing Shirley from the hospital.

A nurse that normally took patients to x-ray, came with the gurney and rolled the patient down the hall, past the nurse's station and to the elevator. X-ray was one floor down, but when the doors closed, the nurse pushed the button marked, basement.

When the doors opened, Toby and Cal were standing ready to help Shirley out of the laundry area onto the service dock and into a black Cadillac Escalade. They settled her in a back seat that was reclined to a position close to that of her hospital bed. The windows of the SUV were totally blacked out, insuring complete privacy. One of Cal's men was waiting outside by the Escalade and helped get Shirley belted into the reclined seat and got in the driver's door, flipping the lock button before starting the powerful V8 into action.

Toby walked to the Camaro and Cal went to a dark blue Toyota Sequoia. Cal took the lead out of the service area and Toby brought up the rear, with the Escalade sandwiched in between. The three car motorcade moved deliberately away from the hospital, careful to avoid any attention by squealing tires or honking of horns.

The caravan turned onto highway 77 until they came to the entrance to Interstate I-35 and then went right onto I-30 west for a few miles. Toby was watching his rear view mirror for any obvious pacing by another vehicle but it was difficult in the afternoon traffic.

They took the 270 degree ramp that turned down onto Walton-Walker Boulevard and headed south. Now the traffic was lighter and Toby was reasonably sure no one was following them.

Cal slowed the pace as the caravan approached a gravel road with no street name. He turned right and about 50' ahead a homemade sign read "*Danger—Unsafe Bridge Ahead—Closed for Repairs.*"

They moved down the road until they came to a bridge with a chain stretched across the approach. Cal stopped the Toyota, got out and loosened the chain and let it fall to the gravel. He waved at Toby and got back in and drove the Sequoia ahead four car lengths. When he had driven over the chain, Toby stopped and got out and lifted the chain to re attach it to the hook on the steel pipe to his left. The chain didn't quite reach the hook, which puzzled Toby because he had just watched Cal unhook it seconds ago. Toby tugged on the chain and it easily moved the distance and when it did, a large, mercury vapor light attached to a nearby tree came on and lit up the gate area. Toby hadn't noticed the light burning when they had approached, or turning off when Cal unhooked the chain.

They drove on down the smoothly graveled road for about half mile and then the headlights unveiled the darkened wood structure at the end of the road. A deep spacious porch spread across the entire front of the house. It was one story but a steep pitched roof and three false dormer windows above the porch, gave the appearance of having a second floor. Security lights on both corners of the house had illuminated the parking area as they pulled up to the house, which Toby now saw was constructed of solid cedar.

He opened the back door of the Escalade and carefully picked Shirley up, out of the vehicle and carried her up the five steps and into the house. When he first saw the large room he had entered, he was shocked. It spanned the entire end of the house from front to back, with hardly any wood framing interfering with the glass wall extending from eight inches above the bamboo floors to an eight inch lateral beam and then more panels of glass filling the arch that led to the "A" framed peak, twenty feet above the floor.

Toby spotted a chaise lounge near and went to set her down. As he loosened his hold on Shirley, his eyes were drawn to the windows. Outside he saw the beautiful waters of a lake, now being colored by the changing hues of fast dying daylight, and stirred by a gentle breeze blowing tiny ripples against the dock that stood sturdily against the movement. He and Shirley were both in a trance, taking in the travel poster scene.

Toby finally spoke, "Think you'll be alright here for a day or two miss? I assure you I'll try to get you back to your duplex as soon as possible."

Shirley just looked up at him with tears forming at the corners of both eyes. "Every time I think I have you figured out, you come up with something new."

Toby sat on the edge of the chaise and took her gently in his arms and held her.

Cal cleared his throat, and said, "Well, I think you two will be all right for now. I don't think anyone followed us and as you saw at the bridge, if anyone drives to the house they will be lit-up at the bridge and there is a control panel, connected to the mercury vapor light, hanging next to the front door that emits a pretty loud whistle and flashes a red blinking light for one minute before it resets.

"There's a master bedroom down the hall from this room. It's located on the other back corner of the house with almost the same view of the lake as you see now. The two doors on the other side of the hall go to two smaller bedrooms. Three bathrooms all together, food in the fridge, and whatever you may want to drink, is in the bar. Oh, and beer is in that fridge. I can leave Sarge; he's your chauffeur, for the night, or have him come back in the morning and relieve you, Toby."

Toby considered what Cal had offered and finally said, "Why doesn't "Sarge" go on back tonight and come back tomorrow. I will need to check in with Perez, in the morning. Maybe I can pick up some vibrations on what may be going on through the Squad."

"OK", said Cal. "By the way, I've arranged for a private nurse to come out and check Shirley and do whatever is required and stay as long as she needs."

Toby reached for Cal's hand and said, "This is all a bit overwhelming, Cal, and I don't know how I'll repay you. This is all way above my pay-grade, but I'll figure some way to pay you back."

Cal took Toby by the shoulders and looked him in the eye. "Don't you give this a second thought, Toby. I can afford this or I wouldn't be here. We're into something that may be bigger than either one of us but I have a feeling that the two of us together can take the bastards. You and Shirley try to get a good night's sleep and we'll talk in the morning. There's a charge cord in the master bath that should charge your cell. It'd be a good idea to plug it in tonight. Call me if you need anything."

Toby watched as the two vehicles moved quietly down the gravel drive. As he came back into the large room and closed the heavy door, the red light started flashing and the whistle filled the house for one minute, then reset to its silent sentry status.

He asked Shirley if he could get her anything.

She said, "Anything grapefruit, if we have it. I'm really thirsty."

Toby poured a grapefruit juice over ice and topped it off with club soda, and mixed his juice with a shot of vodka. He carried the drinks out to the chaise lounge and saw she had moved over and made room for him to join her. He handed her drink over and stretched out next to her, with one arm around her shoulder. They stayed like that for a long time, sipping the drinks and looking at the moon light that was starting to enhance the view of the lake. Shirley dozed off and Toby sat her glass on the floor and just stayed by her, holding her close to his side and wondering where tomorrow was going to lead him.

It was about two in the morning when Shirley stirred and woke Toby. He helped her to the bathroom and went to the closet, where he found a knit shirt that fit her and came almost to her knees. She exchanged her hospital gown for the shirt and Toby helped her to the King sized bed.

"I can't tell you how difficult it's going to be, but I'm going to do my best to stay on my side of the bed. I'm so afraid of putting pressure in the wrong place and aggravating your injuries." Toby said as he tucked the covers around her.

Shirley responded, "Yes, Yes, Yes, stop making excuses and get in bed and I would appreciate it if you would err a little on the side of getting as close as you can without killing me."

They fell back to sleep with her on her back and him curled up as close to her left side as possible with their left hands clasped together.

The next morning, Toby was up early, getting things ready for him to check in with Perez. Shirley had followed doctor's orders and eaten some oatmeal and drank a glass of apple juice. She was sitting up, pretty straight, in bed and Toby was feeling OK about leaving her for a while.

Toby unplugged his cell and called Perez. They arranged to meet in his office at 10:00am.

Toby heard the whistle and saw the red light flashing. He pulled his Glock, and went to a front window. He saw the Escalade pull up in front and Sarge got out and was accompanied by a middle aged woman with shoulder length brown hair. They came in and Sarge introduced the woman as Evelyn, the nurse who would attend to Shirley for as long as she was needed. Shirley liked her right away and Toby's nerve's settled.

While they were all in the bedroom, Toby reviewed the list of concerns with Sarge, Evelyn, and Shirley. That done; he decided he could leave and concentrate on the issues outside the lake-house. He kissed Shirley goodbye, got in the Camaro and began the drive back into town.

CHAPTER 29

PEREZ WAS WAITING IN HIS office when Toby arrived. He was in a foul mood and just pointed Toby to a chair while he finished putting some papers into a folder and filing it in a credenza behind his desk. His mood resulted from a very unpleasant, twenty minute, ass-chewing by Deputy Chief, Ralph Wiggins.

Skip Perez wasn't used to being yelled at by anyone. He'd performed every shitty job Wiggins had ordered, since his unit was formed. He hadn't always understood the orders at the time but he believed in the mission. Because he believed in the mission so strongly he had been able to train his team and gain their confidence to the point, they'd do anything he ordered, without question.

Perez called Wiggins from the scene, after the shooting. This was the one time he'd taken initiative to such a level, without discussing it first. Wiggins was not happy and ordered Perez to pick up the money and bring it to him. He said he'd have to figure out how to cover Perez and his team. So far, Perez had heard nothing further about the money, but it now seemed that Wiggins was hell bent on making Perez the scapegoat for everything. He worried that he couldn't trust Wiggins to look out for the team.

Perez brought his attention back to the situation at hand. He looked across his desk at Toby, and asked, "What's the latest on Shirley? Are you checking on her?"

"Sure Skip, She's still in the hospital, as far as I know. She got hit pretty hard. The doctors say it'll take a while for her to heal up."

Perez continued, "It's a damn shame that a beautiful girl has an accident like that. She's probably lucky it wasn't worse. I read the report, and talked to Traffic. They don't have *lead one* on who might have done it. No witnesses, no clues. If you see her again, tell her we miss her and hope she's back at *Big Jim's* soon."

Toby quietly nodded but didn't say anything.

Perez waved the subject closed and said, "Now, while I was in records, I saw a report on an old buddy of yours. It seems Eddy Sandusky has been released on bail, pending trial. I can't figure how the scumbag was able to make bail but anyway he's back on the street. I'm pretty sure that bullet you put in his right hip has him walking with a distinct limp. He can't be real happy with you. Probably doesn't have the balls to try anything, but you should keep one eye on your back."

Toby was trying to detect any false ring in Perez's words, but just replied, "I appreciate the heads up, Skip. I don't think Sandusky is the type to try a hit on a police officer. He's more of a sneak-thief, if you get my meaning."

"Tell you what, Toby," Perez said, "I'm trying to let things cool down a little. It seems pretty obvious you've gotten involved with Shirley and are concerned about her. You probably want to check on her at the hospital, so why don't you take a couple of days out of the office. Just call in two or three times a day. Then, if anything urgent happens, I can pull you into action with no time lost."

Toby hesitated, then said, "I appreciate the thought, Skip, but I don't know that I will need a lot of time to just call the hospital and check on Shirley. However, my mom is feeling poorly and dad is on a business trip, so I could run out and spend some time with her. Thanks for the PT. I'll call you later this afternoon."

Toby went out to the Camaro before calling Cal. Cal Rodgers told him to come over to his office and he would bring him up to speed.

Rodgers was on the phone when Toby arrived at IBI offices. He waited and listened as Cal finished his call. "OK Stan, that's good stuff. I think we're on the right track. Just keep it going and record everything that's said. Call me every hour or sooner if anything sounds important." He hung up.

"That was one of my agents," Cal said to Toby as he put down the cell. "He's sitting in a van outside Forsythe's office with a tap on his phone and a recorder keeping every word for us to listen to when he gets something important. How did it go at your office?"

Toby gave a brief report on his short visit to see Perez. "It's odd that he offered me some time to check on Shirley. He likes to kid around with her when we're in Big Jim's, but he's not the type to let personal feelings influence him at work. I let him believe Shirley is still in the hospital. The only way he'll know different, is if he goes there to see her or calls to check on her condition."

"Or, if he's the one sending the goon in to kill her," Cal speculated. "Anyway, we have ears on Forsythe and I would feel better if we had eyes on Perez. Do you think you could handle that, without him spotting you?"

"If I had different wheels, I'm sure I could." Toby said.

"That won't be a problem." Cal replied, "I'll get back to you in a minute."

By 11:30am, Toby had parked the dark blue Buick sedan, compliments of International Bureau of Investigation, down the street from the parking lot at the 3rd Precinct. Perez drove a powder blue Firebird and Toby could see it from his location.

At 1:10pm, he called Cal and reported he hadn't seen Perez since he'd arrived on the stakeout.

Cal chuckled and told Toby to have patience. "He's going to move sooner or later, and when he does, you're gonna be on him. Just remember, not too close"

Twenty minutes later, Perez came out the back door and went to the Firebird.

The Firebird's unusual color, made it easy to spot in traffic. Toby was careful to keep the Buick back in the traffic, always two or three cars back from the Firebird.

They didn't drive long before Perez turned the Firebird into the parking lot at *Butch Cassidy's Steak House*. Toby could see the restaurant was on the small side and its reputation was known for serving fine food to a select set of clientele.

Having lunch at a fancy place like *Butch Cassidy's* was a notch above Perez's pay grade and social grouping, Toby was thinking. Toby waited until a group of four came to the door, and then followed them in. Just inside the door was a cozy foyer, separated from the main dining room by an arched opening with a hostess stand next to the arch. Down a short hall to his right, "*Men*" and" *Women*" signs identified the restrooms. Toby waited for the Maitre-d' to show the foursome to a table and then he carefully peered into the elegant dining room.

The room was not crowded. Only five tables were occupied. Two groups of men were having a serious discussion about the pending collapse of the U.S. economy, two other foursomes were still wearing their fashionable golf attire and three women at another table seemed to be catching up on the social gossip as they nibbled on their dessert.

Perez was not in sight at any of the tables. Toby thought about checking the men's toilet, but decided the risk of bumping into Perez and having to explain his being there was a bad idea. He turned and walked out, back to the Buick. A nail shop, hair salon, and tanning shops occupied the property next door and had their own parking lot, separated from *Butch Cassidy's* by a low trimmed hedge. Toby moved the Buick into the neighboring lot and parked next to the hedge. From this vantage point, he had a clear view of the Firebird and *Butch Cassidy's* front door.

Toby called Cal and gave him a report and asked for advice.

Cal thought about what Toby had reported, and said; "I don't think Perez goes to *Butch Cassidy's* and has a $25 lunch and a dry martini all by himself. Keep your eyes on the Firebird and call me when he comes out. Be alert for anyone that comes out with him or right after him. You will need to stay with him until we know if he goes back to work or somewhere else."

It was near 2:00pm when Perez emerged from Cassidy's. He was alone and it didn't appear that he had a lunch buddy. Perez went straight to the Firebird, cranked it up and laid rubber out of the parking lot, onto the street. He headed in the opposite direction from the route he would have taken if he were going back the precinct. Toby followed and called Cal Rodgers.

"You'd better stay with him, Toby." Cal instructed, "Don't get too close, this may be an errand we don't want to miss but we sure don't want you to get burned. I'm puzzled as to why you couldn't see him when you looked in the dining room, but I seem to recall they do have two or three tables in the back part of the dining room that may not be visible from the front. Are you sure no one else came out right after or before him that might have been his companion at lunch?"

"Not while I was looking." Toby said, speeding up to close the gap, as he saw the signal light on the Firebird prepare for a right turn. "Gonna hang up now; he's making a turn into a residential area, I'll call you back when I can."

They had entered a modest, but clean middle-class neighborhood of single family homes. Two more turns and Perez slowed, then stopped in the street and backed into the driveway of a white ranch-style house with a tile roof and stucco walls. He stopped with his trunk close to the two-car garage door, which started to open.

Toby eased to a stop under the spreading limbs of an oak tree, long overdue for a major trim job. He was four houses away from Perez's garage. He could see movement but not clear enough to tell what Perez was doing. Then Perez came out carrying two duffel bags and put them into the trunk of the Firebird. Toby recognized the bags and called Cal.

Cal Rodgers was finishing up a call with his contact at the Port of Galveston when Toby called. "OK Gus, when will you finish processing this shipment and release the container for pick-up? . . . Fine, when that happens, call me on my cell and give me the carrier and when their coming, OK?"

His secretary handed him his opened cell phone. "Hello, Toby? Well my friend, it seems the fat is in the fire and things are starting to pop. What's new on your end?"

"Same situation here, Cal. Our boy just went home and loaded two very special bags in his trunk. They look a lot like the two bags Perez removed from the bank robber's house. I'm following him and currently he's just turned South onto I-45. I hope he's not going all the way to Houston. What do you think?"

"I doubt it Toby," Cal said, "I have confirmed a large container, shipped from Panama and landing in Galveston, is consigned to Forsythe. The destination is Forsythe's warehouse in Ft. Worth. When it clears customs in Galveston, my contact will call me with the name of the truck lines doing the pick-up. Toby, you need to stay with Perez. My guess is he'll deliver the bags somewhere south of Dallas. Forsythe will use the bags to pay for the shipment. We need to know the location for the money delivery. Good luck and be careful."

Toby continued south, down the interstate, keeping the Firebird in sight. A sign read, "Highway 155, Corsicana, I mile."

One minute later, Perez followed the off ramp from the interstate and headed east on 155.

Toby closed the gap between him and Perez and followed the blue Firebird. Soon, another sign read, "Lake Road 1-A, 3 miles. When they came to a cluster of mail boxes mounted on a wooden structure, Perez turned right on 1-A. Toby slowed the Camaro to allow more distance from the Firebird as they wound along the tree shrouded road which found its way down toward the lake until it leveled and turned left where the lake water edged close to the road. Soon they came to a bend, where the water's edge faded away to the right and the road swung left. A narrow drive veered off to the right and led to a log house sitting close to the lakes edge. The drive made a U shape in front and returned to 1-A. A black Chevy Tahoe was sitting along one side of the log structure and Perez stopped the Firebird in front of the steps leading up the front door. The sun had set below the horizon and the light was fading. A porch light flicked on.

Toby had spotted a dirt road going down to a boat launch, and he quickly turned the Buick onto the dirt lane, and killed the motor. He heard a voice in the house call out, "Come on in, and bring the bags." Perez carried the bags up the steps and through the door and the owner of the voice closed the heavy, split log door behind him.

Toby slid out of the Buick and moved silently toward the log house. He could make out a cabin cruiser sitting in the well of the boat-dock. He crept up to a window where he could see part of the main living area. Perez was at the bar, mixing himself a drink. The voice was in the kitchen; I'll be glad to get this business done tonight. I don't think I can tolerate any more mistakes like you made a few nights ago."

Perez raised his voice, "That's not fair. You said in the beginning, I didn't have to check with you every time I needed to take a shit or wipe my ass."

The voice came back, "Taking out a half dozen or more guys in one stroke, is a lot more than going to the bathroom, Mr. Perez.

You have caused me a big headache with that massacre and I don't know how much it's going to cost me to clean up your mess."

Perez questioned, "Cost you? I don't understand. Is somebody making you pay the whole pile of money, just because we killed that bunch of scumbags?"

The voice screamed, "I don't want to hear another fucking word about it. You'll forget the money ever existed if you want to stay healthy."

"What about my men? I'm sure they saw me carry the bags out of the house that night. What if one of them talks out of school?"

The voice was cold as ice, "You've trained those men to do as their told. You can tell them they'll be taken care of when the opportunity presents itself. You can also make it clear that if the wrong people find out about their activities their lives won't be worth the bullet it'll take to shoot them. Now you go on back to town and let me deal with this situation. I'll talk to you in the next day or two and let you know where we go from here."

Toby crawled back into the trees and then ran to the Buick. He backed out onto the lane and drove carefully back to highway 155. He drove east from the turn off a short distance, then did a U-turn onto the shoulder, and turned off the motor and killed the lights. Immediately he saw the lights of the Firebird coming through the trees. Perez turned west toward the interstate.

Toby thought about going back to the lake house, but decided to call Cal first.

"No, Toby, not by yourself. You followed Perez to get information and you got it. Just give me the address of the house on the lake and I'll check out the ownership. You go back to my lake house and relieve Sarge and Evelyn. You've had a pretty productive day."

It was 7:00pm when Toby pulled in at the cedar house on Lake Arlington. When he walked through the front door, he was confronted by the aroma of homemade chili. Sarge was just finishing a bowl and Evelyn was cleaning the kitchen.

Toby walked to the table and inhaled deeply and exclaimed, "Looks like I got here just in time. Boy does that chili smell good!"

Sarge waved him toward the bedroom. "Better check on the patient first. She's been downright cranky the last two hours."

Toby went into the bedroom. Shirley had the drapes opened to provide her a panoramic view of the lake. Her face lit up when she saw him and threw her arms open for him. He pulled her to him and felt the softness and fullness of her. The stresses of the day melted away as she found his lips and kissed him hungrily.

"Wow," he breathed, "if that's what I get every time I come home, I'm going to have to leave more often."

"You try that, mister, and I'll hand-cuff you to the bed. Help me up, I want to go into the living room."

Toby hesitated, "Do you think you should? Are you strong enough?"

Shirley put her hands on her hips, "What's going on? Do you have some other girl hidden out there you don't want me to see?"

Toby put one of her arms around his neck and supported her around the waist, then looked at her and asked; "Are you ready to try this?"

Shirley said, "If you move that hand up about ten inches higher, I could be ready to try anything." She laughed at herself and then coughed and grimaced.

Toby scolded her, "Behave yourself woman before I put you back in bed."

"Promises, promises, promises," Shirley said as they made their way out to the great-room.

She sat and watched him eat his chili, while Sarge and Evelyn prepared to leave.

"Anything happen here today?" Toby asked, as they headed for the door.

"Nothing but the snoring from the bedroom," Sarge said, grinning. "I don't expect anyone to track this place. Cal's got it covered pretty well on the title at the county records. You guys just have a nice evening. You'll hear from Cal sometime this evening. They got in their vehicle and drove away. Thirty seconds later, the whistle and flashing light started.

Toby had another bowl of chili and remembered he hadn't eaten much all day. Shirley found a deck of cards and they played gin-rummy until she complained of being tired, then Toby helped her to the chaise lounge and they sat and held each other for a long time. They went to bed early—and after much experimenting, they found a way to lie together, holding one another very closely, and fell asleep.

Toby woke up about 3:00am and checked the place over. He used the charge cord Cal had told him about and plugged his cell phone into the wall by the night stand, and went back to bed. He was just dozing off when he heard the sound. Something moving on the back deck, then he heard a scratching sound. He rose up and slid out of the bed, taking the Glock from the night stand and walked to the back door. He quietly turned the dead-bolt with his free hand, and then gripped the door handle, he put his forefinger of his gun hand under the light switch and he was ready. With one move, he pulled the door opened and flooded the back porch with light just in time to see the adult skunk and three babies scamper across the deck and duck under the steps, leaving a terrible stink behind.

When he went back to the bedroom, Shirley was sitting up in the bed. He told her what had happened in vivid detail and had to stop because she was laughing so hard she was hurting herself.

He got back in bed and she came to him, with her mouth close to his ear and said in a whisper, "Is it OK if I say I think I love you?"

The next morning, they woke in the same position as when Shirley had whispered in his ear. The words came back to him and Toby didn't find them uncomfortable. Before he said anything to her, his phone gave off its shrill ring.

"Hello!" he said as he sat on the side of the bed. "Good morning Cal," Yes, everything is OK here. We had a quiet night and haven't gotten out of bed yet. . . . No, it's OK, we are awake and I would've called you soon. What's up?

Toby sat on the bed and nodded his head and made one syllable responses for five minutes or more. Finally he said, "OK Cal, we'll wait here and see you in about an hour."

When Cal arrived, he had Sarge and another agent named Luis with him. Introductions were made all around.

Cal motioned for Toby to follow him into the kitchen. "Toby, are there any good guys you can recruit from the PPD that would join us on a trip to the lake house near Corsicana, tonight?"

Toby thought, and said, "Two or three, I can think of. Want me to call them and see if their available and willing?"

Cal spoke in a low voice, "My thinking is that Forsythe took delivery of the bank money. He probably arrived after you left last night or this morning. The man who met Perez probably wasn't Forsythe. That man has probably been the contact between Perez and Forsythe all along, but now that the money is being moved, Forsythe will want to be in on the action. Forsythe needs something he can sell legitimately on this end to convert the bank money to *untraceable money*. He has an import/export company and that can justify buying something in South America, Panama, or Mexico that might be legitimately or illegitimately owned in its source country but perfectly legal for him to own it here. The only thing illegal and traceable here is the stolen money and that's hard to prove without your testimony. The shipment is scheduled to be delivered to his warehouse in Ft. Worth, but I'm sure the payment for the shipment will take place at the lake. We don't know how many men will show up to receive the money but I'd bet it won't be just one. I'm thinking we need four or five guys. We stake out the house and when the money is delivered, we take over the meeting."

Toby didn't say anything. He didn't disagree with Cal but he was having trouble digesting all the details. He asked, "Cal, what do you suspect is in that shipment?"

"That's the six to seven hundred thousand dollar question. If it's legitimate, like art or other collectables, then the question is: are they stolen? If they are legit, then Forsythe will take a major discount in the laundry. If, on the other hand, it is illegal, it may move at a big mark up. Six hundred thousand dollars could become one or two million if the right commodity is being bought and sold." Cal slapped the kitchen table and said, "We won't know until we get out there. I need you and your recruits back here by one o'clock. Good luck, and remember, these guys need to be handy with a gun and not afraid to use one."

Toby hugged Shirley and assured her that she would be okay until he returned and then this nightmare would be over. He left Sarge and Evelyn to watch over Shirley and headed back into the city.

Toby called Sonny as he drove and arranged to meet him at the *Dunkin Donuts* near Sonny's apartment. When Toby arrived, Sonny was in a booth, nursing a cup of coffee and another was waiting for Toby.

"I didn't get donuts. Don't know about you, but my stomach is beginning to look like I'm storing up for a long, cold winter," Sonny said, as he reached to shake hands.

"I don't need the calories either." Toby took a big swallow of coffee and spoke in a low voice, "What I'm about to tell you is in strictest confidence. If, after I confide in you, you decide you can't help me, I will move on and never bring the subject up again, and no hard feelings. OK?"

Sonny said, "Cut the dramatics and get on with what you want me to do."

About ten minutes later, Toby finished and asked the waitress to warm up his coffee.

When she'd walked away from their table, Sonny whistled softly and then said, "I'll say this for you, partner, when you look for trouble, you don't mess around with Abilene. No sir, you go straight to Dallas. The lucky thing for you is that this is my day off and I was wondering what I would do to fight off the boredom, and here you are with the answer."

Toby reached across the table and covered both of Sonny's hands with his, and said, "Sonny this could get rough so be sure before you commit."

Sonny scratched his head and said, "I don't recall you giving me any choice when we went into the alley behind Harold's Drugs a few months back. Did I miss something?"

Toby squeezed Sonny's hands. "You didn't miss a thing, partner. Do you need to go back home and pick up anything?"

"Everything I'll need is in my truck. Vest, two hand guns, and I threw in a short barrel 12 gauge, just in case."

"You had an idea what I wanted?" Toby asked

Sonny smiled. "I read you like a book. Let me grab my gear and let's get out of here before I change my mind."

They met Ron Perry in the parking lot of Safeway where he had been shopping when Toby called him. They sat at an outdoor table meant for customers of the Starbuck counter just inside the grocery. Toby repeated the story he'd told Sonny and then just shut up and looked his training officer in the eye.

"Son of a bitch, Toby!" Perry said. "You have stepped into a very, large pile-of-shit. There are all kinds of legal questions and I'm no attorney. What happens when the bad guys decide to tell you to go *fuck yourself* and start defending that pile of money?"

Toby thought carefully. "I don't think it will be much different than Eddy Sandusky defending his bag of pills. Somebody's going to get shot."

"We'll it's my day off, and if I want to spend some time with one of my slower learning trainees, reinforcing his basic understanding of police work, it's my business."

They followed Perry to his house and waited while he brought out a set of equipment similar to Sonny's.

Toby's phone chirped. It was Cal. "Toby, a change in battle plans. How's your recruiting coming?"

"Me, and two of PPDs finest are packed and ready to go to your lake house." Toby slowed and pulled to the curb.

"That's the change Toby; we're gonna meet at the *Circle T Truck Stop* on the interstate south of Dallas. It's about half way to the turn off to the Corsicana lake house. Time table is moving up. Tell you more when I see you."

Toby pulled in at The Circle T, about 1:30pm, and saw Cal's rig near the restaurant entrance. He and his recruits went inside and he spotted Cal and two men he didn't recognize seated at a round table. One of the men, Otto, looked to be in his late thirty's, 6'1" carrying 190 pounds of lean hardened muscle. Otto shaved his head closer than Toby shaved his face, and sported a bushy black mustache. He carried himself like he was still military, ready for inspection.

The other man was called Stan, and he was the opposite of Otto. Stan had long brown hair, pulled into a pony tail, looked 30 pounds overweight but with hardness underneath and was sloppy in his mismatched clothes. Stan had pale blue eyes that moved constantly as if recording everything they saw and instantly sending the image to the brain for processing for quick reaction to any danger signals.

Then, a smiling Mexican man came out of the men's room and came to their table. He sat down next to Stan.

Cal said, "Augustine say hello and then forget you ever saw this motley crew."

Augustine laughed and said, "Sí, sí mi amigo.

Cal Added, "Augustine will not be part of the strike force, but if my theory is correct, he will have an important job after we have control of the situation."

When introductions were complete Sarge walked up and took the last remaining chair.

Toby's alarm bell went off. "Sarge, I thought you were supposed to be with Shirley?"

Cal answered, "Evelyn is with Shirley, and I doubt if our friends will be searching for her tonight, with all the activities they have planned. As soon as we have everything under control, you can dash back to the lake and take care of her."

The thinking made sense, so Toby forced himself to relax a little and focus on the briefing Cal was conducting.

Cal had obtained information from T-M Truck Lines that the shipment from Galveston would arrive in Ft. Worth about 3:30 or 4:00pm this afternoon. The driver had a phone number he was to call and get the shippers permission to complete the delivery. If the shipper refused permission, the driver was to take the trailer to T-Ms terminal in Ft. Worth and hold it until further instructions were received.

CHAPTER 30

TWO HUNDRED FIFTY MILES TO the south in the town of Piedras Negras, Mexico, Jorge Cortez and Pablo Santiago were driving up to the check point at the crossing of the Rio Grande River. On the other side of the bridge was the flip side of Piedras Negras, located in Texas. Except for the bridge and the wide river-bed that provided passage for the narrow stream that flowed this time of year, the two towns could be merged together and a visitor would be hard-pressed to tell where one stopped and the other started. The citizens of both towns considered the bridge and the cursory check, done by the border guards, more of a nuisance than anything else. They all crossed the river daily to go to work and conduct commerce with each other. The Texas side was heavily populated by Mexican families and there had been a sizable number of gringos on the Mexico side, in spite of the violence that had erupted from the rivalry that flared between groups within the cartel.

Five years ago they practically walked across the bridge without slowing down. Then the drugs began to move in larger volume. Then the economy in Mexico deteriorated to unsurviveable proportions. There was no work, and in Mexico if you didn't work; you didn't eat. Then the people began to cross the shallow river one way and not come back, the way they had traditionally.

Then the cartels began to seize the economic advantage presented by both activities. Helping people in the processing of their daily challenges and reaping a profit was soon not enough. Ruthless men began to organize the activities into volumes of enterprise; kidnappings on both sides of the Rio Grande, human smuggling, and narcotics trafficking were the most common activities. No one interfered with the control the cartels exercised and anyone who tried was executed along with members of their families. Power and wealth were the only motives that mattered and a complete disregard for human life made the guidelines for decisions on policy very simple.

Jorge and Pablo had initially been competitors but quickly understood that there was enough to make both of them rich and powerful. They complimented one another in their abilities and resources. They reasoned that it was better for both of them to gain immense wealth and yet work together to build the power to protect that wealth from others who would wrench it from them. They had accomplished most all of their ambitions and except for unauthorized outburst of violence between small groups that didn't like one another to begin with, the pair had kept the lid on and built one of the most powerful and effective cartels along the Tex-Mex border.

In the business of drugs and human trafficking and assorted other criminal activities that came with them, friendship did not matter and would never determine behavior. Self-interest was the lone factor that determined actions and reactions and that's what led Jorge and Pablo to the bridge to cross over into Texas.

Jorge and Pablo were doing something unusual today. They were driving themselves in one of their fleet of black Chevrolet Tahoes. Normally they would have been traveling separately, each in the back seat with a driver and two bodyguards.

Their zapateria in Piedras Negras was their legitimate business and it served its good purpose when they needed a good cover for going in and out of the United States. They carried shoes from Europe and Latin America and Justin cowboy boots from Texas. They traveled to El Paso to select the latest designs and order them shipped to their Zapeteria. To satisfy the curiosity of the border guards, the two cartel captains brought back about 50 pair in the Tahoe to convince them they had truly been on a boot buying trip.

Just as they were coming to the edge of town where they were approaching the highway that led north to El Paso, Pablo turned south toward Carrizo Springs. Just outside the little town, Pablo pulled up to a gate with a sign that read, "Flying Feather Sport Farm." For a few months in the winter this 5000 acres of south Texas, with its scattered, flooded lowlands, became home to endless flocks of Canadian Geese and four or five varieties of ducks, all coming south for the winter.

Hunters from the states to the north and east flew in and landed on the private air strip and tested their ability with an assortment of shotguns. It was an opportunity for thousands of corporate executives to escape the reality of their work, bring key clients and customers and imagine they were back to the past when man braved the challenges of their environment and harvested food from the bountiful supply mother-nature had supplied. Jorge and Pablo had recognized the strategic value of the game farm, five years ago and purchased it in the name of an El Paso Corporation they had formed. Now the dry hot summer prevailed and until the rains and hunters returned, the farm was closed and abandoned.

Jorge keyed the lock on the gate and re-locked it after Pablo drove the Tahoe through. When they got to the airstrip, a Cessna 210 was sitting at the end of the runway with motors running at idle. They climbed aboard and the pilot eased the throttles forward and began to move the plane down the runway. At 70mph, he pulled back on the yoke and the plane rose into the Texas sky. The pilot adjusted course and headed toward Waco.

There was no traffic around the small, unattended airport east of Waco. The landing was uneventful and they taxied up to six men standing in front of two black Tahoes, identical to the one they had left back at the ranch.

Jorge and Pablo rarely traveled together and they seldom traveled into the United States except for their perfunctory trips to San Antonio. They were both apprehensive about the delivery of and payment for the shipment from Panama. They were dealing with the man Forsythe, for the first time and it was a significant sale for a first transaction. Neither one of the partners trusted the other to close the deal and pick up the money. They felt that all reasonable safeguards had been taken and thought the plan to take the money back to Piedras Negras was as foolproof as they could make it. The trip to buy boots had never failed to work with their friends at the border crossing.

They each got into a separate Tahoe with a driver and two body guards. These men were totally trustworthy and seasoned in their duties. They instructed them on the route to Forsythe's log house on the lake. It was a beautiful day for a drive in Texas, but both men harbored a feeling of dread that would only go away when they returned to the comfort of their homes and the safety of their army of protectors. They were about an hour away from the lake house, near Corsicana.

CHAPTER 31

EVERYONE HAD LOADED THEIR EQUIPMENT into the two SUVs, and headed toward the Corsicana Lake. During the drive, Toby was thinking about the theory Cal had presented yesterday. It appeared that Cal's hunches could be right-on-the-money. Toby was riding in the front with Cal. On the way, Cal reported that his girl in his office had confirmed the lake house belonged to the import/export company registered in Panama. "It's a sure thing the sellers of the shipment will come there sometime before 3:30pm to pick up the money. We need to be in positions well before then."

At the lake, the vehicles moved slowly, avoiding any noise that would be heard in the log house. They eased the vehicles into the lane leading to the boat ramp, and pulled into two cleared places cut out of the brush for trucks and boat trailers to be parked out of the way of other boaters who may come later to launch their boats. Otto pulled out two green and brown camouflage netting and covered each SUV.

Cal had a plot map of the property and had marked each mans location. He pulled out a bag containing small walkie-talkies and handed one to each man. The number on the communicator matched the number of his assigned position on the map. He handed each man a red armband to make sure they didn't get into a friendly-fire incident.

Cal raised his hand and said softly, "If we can do this without any shooting, that's good, but remember, you are the good guys and above all, I don't want anyone of you to get hurt. You know what the job is, so let's go do it. You're all professionals, if someone has to get hurt, make sure it's them, not us."

The seven men melted into the woods and found their way to their assigned post. It was 2:45pm.

They had barely had time to settle in their locations when they heard a door slam and a car start and drive down the gravel road, away from the log house. Toby was in the best position near the road and he jotted down the Texas plate number as the dark blue Lincoln disappeared around a curve.

Voices came over the walkie-talkies. Did everybody leave? Did we miss the action?

Cal's calm voice said, "Settle down everybody. Toby, did you get the plates?"

"Yeah Cal, I got it all and there was a small tag on the windshield; lower left corner. I couldn't read it but it was like a parking permit or identifier of some kind." Toby answered.

Each man returned to his task and took a few minutes to select the vantage point that presented the best view of their portion of the log house.

Otto and Stan had each brought *Bushmaster* .223 caliber rifles. They were auto loading, with high velocity ammunition that stopped a man in mid-sentence; if hit in the right place, before there was time to react to an alarm. Sonny and Ron had *Remington* 12 gauge shotguns and the rest had *Glocks* except Sarge who had a *Mac 10* slung under his right shoulder.

They sat in their hiding places and waited; still; not moving. They tuned their ears to all the noises that were part of nature filling the forest with the breathing and microscopic movements of creatures unseen.

Then it was all interrupted by the sound of tires crunching the gravel and the heavy motor's pushing vehicles toward the log house. Then they detected the first sign of life in the house.

A pair of Chevy Tahoes came into view. They were black, with totally blacked out windows, sporting Texas license plates. Two men, carrying *Uzi* machine guns got out of each vehicle and took up positions beside the rear passenger doors and waited. They had dark brown skin with thick black hair and speaking snatches of Spanish. The front door of the house opened, and Forsythe came out on the porch and waved, apparently, to someone still in the vehicles.

Two of the security men moved to open a back door on each Tahoe. Jorge Cortez and Pablo Santiago emerged and were immediately protected by the armed men waiting for them. Both men wore mocha brown pants of fine material and tailored to fit perfectly, flared slightly over the western style, snakeskin boots. They each had on identical dark brown, thigh length, leather coats that hid most of the skin tight, western silk shirts, fastened up the front with pearl covered snaps.

Both men appeared in perfect physical condition and moved with arrogance in their step and carriage.

Walter Forsythe moved down the steps and extended his right hand. "Hola Amigo, welcome to my home. You have driven far today and you must be thirsty. Please come inside and refresh yourselves."

Two of the security men went into the house ahead of the two commanders, and then motioned to them that it was ok.

Toby, Sonny, Cal, and Ron Perry were slowly working their way through the low growing foliage, toward the house. Toby had reached a sheltered spot behind a full shaped brush. He realized a nearby window was opened slightly allowing him to hear the conversation inside clearly.

Two of the sentries remained outside the log house and very alert to their surroundings. One of them suddenly straightened and looked toward the trees. Cal was squirming past a flowering bush, causing it to vibrate noticeably. The Mexican kept moving toward Cal and began to pull his Uzi up to point it in his direction.

Toby heard the "huff" sound from the silenced Bushmaster, back in the trees, and saw a red welt appear in the middle of the sentry's forehead. The Mexican's mouth opened but made no sound as he crumpled to the ground. Now, Stan began to more aggressively change his position in relation to the SUVs.

Toby was watching the other security man who was now looking around for his companion. He came around the side of the house where he last saw his buddy. The "huff" sound re-occurred and the man's throat exploded as the slender bullet tore through the cartilage of his throat, taking out a chunk of his spinal column as it exited. He dropped like a wet sheet falling off the clothes line.

The driver of the lead Tahoe caught sight of the falling man from the corner of his eye. He opened his door and called out, "Miguel, are you okay?" The high-speed bullet went into his opened mouth and came out through his neck, just below the base of his skull.

A loud voice—sounding the alarm—was heard inside the log house.

Sonny Montgomery and Ron Perry mounted two steps and crashed through the back door simultaneous with Toby and Cal Rogers entering thru the front. The two security men were back to back firing their automatic Uzi's at windows and doors. Toby and Cal dived behind furniture in opposite directions. Toby rolled to his right and squeezed a volley of shots from his Glock. One of the security men went down screaming.

The older of the two commanders pulled a heavy-caliber pistol from under his leather coat and with a stream of profanity spewing from his mouth; he fired four shots, almost point blank at a bewildered Walter Forsythe, who died with a questioning look etched in his face. The remaining commander and his last security protector ran toward the front door, luckily opened. At the last second they both turned to fire retreating cover. Ron Perry and Sonny Montgomery fired two blasts from their shotguns that seemed to push the two Mexicans back through the opening as if they were caught by a gust of wind.

There was an eerie silence through the house. The men that were still alive were wiping their eyes in response to the strong smell of burned gunpowder. Otto and Stan came in the back door and Toby saw Sarge through a window, checking the dead driver by the Tahoe.

Cal looked around the interior at the coughing men. Not one appeared to be wounded. Unbelievable, he thought.

"Well, so much for taking them without firing a fucking shot."

Someone chuckled, and then another, and then they all began to laugh uncontrollably.

When the laughter settled and stopped, Cal turned to face them. He spoke in a firm voice, "I don't know if any of you were using your service firearms that could be traced. Ron and Sonny were using shotguns so they're clean. My men were using throw away pieces. Toby, I saw you holding a Glock, is that PD issued?"

"No Cal, it's left over from a melt—down that went bad. It's clean, but I'll lose it anyway."

Cal went on, "OK, now Toby, go fetch Augustine at the vehicles and tell him to hurry, and I want someone to search the two Mexican cowboys for cell phones and bring them to me."

In five minutes, Cal had both cell phones. They had been in the side pockets of the leather coats and had amazingly escaped the blasts from the shotguns. Augustine arrived and Cal barely finished briefing him before one of the cell phones started ringing.

Cal let the cell ring three times before letting Augustine answer. It wasn't as much a long-shot as Cal had feared when the idea first occurred to him. The truck driver was Mexican but not part of the gang. He was supposed to call the number and ask, in Spanish, if he should let them unload the cargo. Augustine answered the phone in Spanish and when the voice asked him if everything was okay to complete the delivery, Augustine said 'sí' as enthusiastically as if he was counting the bags full of money and putting it into his own bank account.

After the call, Cal called the team together and asked, "How many of you are still in? We may be at this for the rest of the night." Every hand went up!

"OK," Cal said, "If your gun is totally clean, consider leaving it here. We're going to call in an anonymous tip, and when the police come and find more guns than shooters, it will confuse the scene. They may conclude that some shooters escaped and left their guns behind."

They made sure there was nothing left at the scene that could tie their presence to the grizzly scene. When they were satisfied the scene was sterile of their presence. They loaded into the vehicles and drove away from the log house. They stopped at the Circle T and picked up the vehicles they'd left on their way down. It now seemed like their meeting earlier in the day had happened a long time ago.

Toby called Shirley and was relieved to hear her voice sounding stronger, but full of concern when he told her they had one more stop to make and it might take all night.

Toby lowered his voice, and said, "Do you remember the question you asked me just after I got up and saved you from a horrible fate, lurking in the dark? I've decided it's OK!"

Shirley smiled from ear to ear, and set the phone down, gently.

Toby didn't miss the fact that Shirley hung up the phone without saying anything. Then he turned and said, "Cal, I'm just remembering the car that drove away right after we got into position at the lake house. Any idea who that might be?"

Cal was looking out at the headlights cutting into the black of the night on the freeway and answered, "I don't have a name, Toby, but I have been rolling some thoughts around in my head. It's like the voice we heard at the lake house, but never saw the person speaking. It's interesting that this individual likes to get-out-of-dodge before anything happens. Like the guy—well, I assume it was a guy—who met Perez for lunch but you couldn't see him. I don't know his name but the bastard sure is shy. Right now we have to just follow the leads and go where they take us. Next stop is Forsythe's warehouse!"

The caravan pulled into the industrial park about 8:00PM and drove around back, once they verified the address, and the name *Gulf Trading Partners, SA*. Most of the warehouses in the development had small offices across the front leaving 90% of the space as warehouse space. In the rear there was a truck-high dock and a pedestrian door next to the overhead door. It took less than a minute to pick the lock on the small door. Toby used a small flashlight to find the breaker box and turn on the large, mercury lights overhead.

The shipment was in cardboard boxes, put into rows, five boxes high. Each box had "FRAGILE" stamped all over the boxes, so no one could miss it. They opened one of the boxes and found four pottery pieces in the shape of artistic birds about a foot tall; like the ones people painted at the time-share condos all over Mexico and other exotic resorts across Latin America and the Caribbean. Cal set one of the figures out on the table, put down the box cutter and pulled out his gun, holding it by the barrel; he struck the ceramic with the butt. The fragile ceramic bird shattered and the fragments lay in a heap of odd pieces.

"That'll teach the bastard; you broke one of his birds," Toby joked.

Cal smiled as he reached back into the box, and said grimly; "I may have to break a lot more to find what I'm looking for."

Cal smashed two more birds with the same result, but when he struck the fourth one, the breaking sound was different; it broke into fewer pieces. Among the larger pieces was a packet made of brown, waxy paper about 4" square, sealed tightly with duct tape.

Otto leaned over and picked up the packet, cut it open with the box cutter and dipped some of the white powder onto his tongue, "That's pretty good stuff, he finally said. Quality enough it can be cut two or three times before it hits the street. Have to weigh it to be sure but looks like a ¼ or ½ a kilo. My guess is there is one loaded chicken in each box. Lowers the risk a box will accidently break open or customs will check the right piece of pottery."

Cal spoke, "Any way you figure it, we've got a shit-load worth of Cocaine here."

"What are we going to do with it Cal?" Asked Otto

"Turn it and the money over to The Feds," Said Cal, "The question is: WHEN! We've still got one or two fish to catch and this is excellent bait."

They finished at the warehouse by 9:30pm after opening a number of the boxes and convincing themselves they had a major drug bust on their hands.

Toby returned Cal's Buick and climbed into the Camaro and headed toward Lake Arlington.

He dialed Shirley's number on the cell. "Hey lady, I decided to run away earlier tonight, but when I got half way to Florida, I began to imagine what you must look like in a bikini on a Florida beach, so I turned around and came back, and I'll be there in twenty minutes."

Shirley giggled and said, "Well, I have to tell you, you're too late. I had my bikini on for two hours, waiting for you. I finally gave up on you and took it off."

"In that case, I'll be there in five minutes, don't do a thing till I get there." Toby punched off the cell.

Toby pulled the Camaro up to the Cedar House, on Lake Arlington seven minutes later. He walked into the great-room and saw Evelyn asleep on the couch.

"In here," he heard Shirley say. He walked back to the bedroom and found her as she promised. Her bikini was off and she was sitting up in the bed.

"Miss, you will catch a cold if you don't put some clothes on!"

"I can't do that by myself. Maybe you should get undressed and get over here and keep me warm." Shirley slid down under the sheet.

Toby was under the sheet in seconds.

The next morning, he opened his eyes and saw hers looking straight into his.

He moved his face closer and kissed her deep and she moved against him, and then followed as she rolled with him onto his back. She reached down and slid him inside her, rocking back and forward until they both reached an exhilarating climax together. She lay back down on his stomach and he rolled her back onto the sheet. They lay still for a while, until their breathing slowed, then turned toward each other again, and in unison said, "Wow."

Toby could hear Evelyn moving about in the kitchen. He got out of bed and started the shower. Shirley joined him, and they slowly refreshed themselves and *drank in* the intimacy they had become so comfortable with.

Toby was toweling off when he heard his phone.

"Toby, It's Skip Perez. "I want to see you in my office this morning. Is Shirley still in the hospital?"

Toby sensed Perez was asking a question, he already knew the answer to.

"No Skip, I brought her home last night. She's feeling much better, but I stayed at her place just to make sure she got a good night's sleep. I think she's going to be OK now. What time at your office?"

Perez hesitated, then said, "Take two hours, I'll see you at 10:00, don't be late."

Toby broke the connection and hit his speed dial for Cal Rogers.

"Cal, this is Toby, something may be developing. Perez wants me in his office at 10:00am, and he asked about Shirley. He wanted to know if she was still in the hospital, but I have a feeling he already knew she wasn't. Something is happening. I can feel it."

Cal was quiet for a moment then said, "You're probably right. I wonder if he got a tip about the lake house shooting. Maybe he tried to contact Walter Forsythe, and when he couldn't, he's putting together some help to go down to the lake and check it out. You're the newest and youngest member of his team. He might see you as the most gullible and expendable if he finds trouble when he gets there. You go meet him and follow his lead, whatever he wants. Sarge is here in the office. I'm going to take him and head down to the lake. I should have secured the cash last night. My thinking was that we would tip the Feds and let them find it where it was; like no one had touched it after the shooting. But, I don't want to risk having Perez make off with it and making it disappear. The money is our key to tying all the events and characters together."

"OK Cal, if Perez wants me to go with him and we head south toward the lake, do I go-with-the-flow whatever develops?"

"Yes Toby, that's exactly what you do. Remember, you're still part of Perez's team, so play the part, right up to the point you begin to put yourself in mortal danger. If Perez gets on the interstate highway, headed south, you tell Perez you need to call Shirley and tell her you'll see her tonight. You actually call me, and pretend I'm Shirley. We'll know you're coming and be prepared to welcome you properly.

CHAPTER 32

FIVE MEN SAT AROUND THE conference table in the small room used by the mayor for meetings. The location of this room assured him the least amount of scrutiny from the public, press, and even city employees who were always scurrying about, performing their urgent, (but ultimately not terribly important) errands.

Mayor Summers; Council President, Troy Taylor; Police Chief, Cameron Walker; and City Attorney, Rodney Dawson had met together in the room on many occasions. The room sat just behind Mayor Summer's private office with one door connecting the two, and another opening out to the corridor, leading to the back stairs in city hall. It was the first time in the room for the fifth man. FBI agent Terry Marks, a resident agent in the Dallas Office, and head of the task force, investigating the bank robberies was closely perusing the mahogany paneled walls and ceiling. The doors were solid, six panel wood construction and there were no windows. Marks thought it was almost a duplication of an interrogation room in the Federal Court House, (except the one at the Court House had CCTV cameras in each corner at the ceiling level).

A coffee carafe sat in front of each attendee. Mayor Summers started the meeting. "I do appreciate everyone being here, especially you, Agent Marks. I'm sure your schedule is frantic and it is especially generous of you to come here and give us an opportunity to get up to speed on where The Task Force is on the investigation is at this point. I also welcome this opportunity to communicate the concern we and everyone in the area has for the apprehension of these cold blooded robbers and killers. We are charged with the duty of assuring the citizens of our communities they can sleep safe in their beds at night."

Terry Marks had heard remarks like this from politicians in Washington DC, Atlanta, and now from the boys in Plainfield, Texas. He knew the election for city offices was coming around in less than a year and as the campaigns drew nearer, and the robbers remained at large, these meetings would become more numerous and more unpleasant.

Each man echoed the mayor's comments and when they were finished, Marks replied, "Gentlemen, I want to assure you that every law enforcement officer, The FBI, and many others are working night and day on this investigation. It is most unusual that we have not developed more leads at this stage of the investigation. None of the money has surfaced, and no new robberies have occurred. It's like they came out of the ground, robbed two banks and ran back into their boroughs, underground and hibernated for the winter. Let me assure each of you, we will catch them! The leads have been slim but we have some, and teams are running down each one. I hope to have better news later this week."

"Is there anything you can give us today?" Asked Chief Summers.

Marks pushed back his chair, "No, and I caution you to be careful about talking to the press at this time. Speculation, seen or heard by the robbers can only help them continue to avoid out attention. I have another meeting to attend, but I promise to update you with any important breakthroughs in the case."

They men shook hands and Marks exited the room and headed down the hall to the back stairs. He was just getting into his government issued Chevy, when his cell vibrated at his belt.

He didn't recognize the calling number, but acted on a hunch and pushed the button and said hello.

"Agent Marks, this is Calvin Rogers with the International Bureau of Investigation. You may be familiar with our firm here in the DFW area. Also you and I met after you spoke to the American Society for Industrial Security Convention, last fall in New Orleans."

Marks thought carefully. "Yes Mr. Rogers, what can I do for you?"

"It's more what I can do for you, Mr. Marks. If you can spare me two or three hours I think I can help you close the file on the recent bank robberies." Cal stated with confidence.

Weeks made a chuckling sound and said, "Mr. Rogers, I have twenty plus people working overtime on that investigation, and two or three hours of my time are being sought by a mob of important people. Why should I drop everything and chase after some theory of yours?"

"It's more than a theory, Mister Marks, and speaking of important people, some of them are in this crime up to their eye balls. And some of them are dead!" Cal Rogers emphasized the last words and let silence hang over them for effect.

Eventually Marks spoke, "You're tone implies you are sure of what you're saying, but so far, I don't have any specifics to help me believe you know anything."

Cal spoke softly, "Agent marks, what little I know about you indicates you're a dedicated professional. Six years with Marine Force Recon, Thailand and Cambodia during Vietnam. Law degree from George Washington University after the war and joined the FBI. You've had two routine assignments with the Bureau and came out of both with citations for outstanding service. You're smart in ways most Special Agents are not. If I tell you everything I know, then you're going to have the ability to hurt some people that shouldn't be hurt. You're also going to be able to recover most of the stolen money for the FDIC and hurt some people that deserve to be hurt but won't be without my help. I hope you're going to be able to look past some things and use your wisdom and experience when you hear what I'm going to share with you. Are you available and interested?"

Agent Marks was silent for a moment before he said, "Cal, you and I have known each other long enough for you to know the answer to that question. I am always interested in recovering federally insured money stolen from a bank and I won't rest until I catch the bastard that disfigured one teller and killed another. What do you have?"

CHAPTER 33

TOBY DROVE THE CAMARO INTO the large parking area of the *Circle T.* It was mid afternoon and traffic was light. Toby spotted the Tahoe Perez was driving, off to the right and pulled along-side, rolling down the window and nodding hello. Toby recognized Tyler, sitting in the back of the Tahoe.

Perez nodded back and said, "Park it and get in, we'll go in mine."

Without further words, they pulled onto the interstate and headed south.

A couple of miles down the road, Toby turned in his seat where he could see both of his traveling companions and asked, "What's up guys, where we going?"

"We're going out here in fucking nowhere and take care of some unfinished business. That's what's up and that's where we're going. You, ever, been down here before, Toby?" Perez questioned through clinched teeth.

Toby thought carefully, "I'm not sure, Skip. Isn't this the Interstate that goes down to Houston?"

"That's right, it goes down to Huston. Ever been to Houston, Toby?"

"Yeah," Toby said. "I rode down here with some buddies and went fishing out of a marina near Galveston. Didn't do any good though; a lot of heat, humidity, and no fish, as I recall."

"Well, we ain't going all the way to Huston; but you could say we're going fishing, sort of. The kind of fish we're after, today mostly walks around on two legs. You're sure; you've never been down here before?"

"I've never been a lot of places before, Skip, just college, the Academy and here on the job for about 18 months. I haven't gotten around to the rest of the world yet. Why are you being so mysterious about where were going today?" Toby was looking out the side window at landmarks.

Perez began to reduce his speed as he said, "You got a lot to learn, Roberts, and I don't like people getting educated at my expense. You know what I mean?"

Toby played the cat and mouse game, "No, Skip, I can't say I do know what you mean. Just tell me straight out."

Perez spoke through clenched teeth, "You've only been on my team a short time, but we've already done some heavy duty work and I don't have any complaints about you pulling your load. This bank robber stuff is different than anything we've gotten into before, and we took a giant step out of bounds on it. By the time we got evidence, it was tainted beyond being useful in court. If we had tried to hand it off to others, the bad guys would have slipped away from all of us, scot-free! The way some of the aspects of that operation were handled makes me all queasy and feeling hung out to dry. I'm willing to give a lot to the job and bend, or even break a few rules, but I do draw the line on certain principles. First principal is this. Whatever else I may have done, I am not a thief, and I don't like being hung out to dry, looking like one."

Perez slowed down and turned off onto State road #155 and headed toward the lake. Toby tensed and asked, "Where in the hell are we going, Skip?"

"Checking out a house up ahead. We're going in as quiet as possible but be prepared for trouble. We must not let anyone take control of the situation, no matter who they are or what they say. Are you clear?" Perez said as he slowed the truck to a crawl and turned into the drive to the boat launch. He stopped the vehicle and sat quiet."

Tyler leaned forward and whispered, "Boss, I don't hear a sound. Do we go on foot?"

They got out and began to make their way through the trees, soon catching sight of the roofline of a house. The foliage cleared enough to see the log house and back yard trailing down to the lake. No sign or sounds of life welcomed their approach. Perez motioned for Tyler and Toby to spread out and approach the house from three directions. Perez moved toward the front area and saw three vehicles sitting at odd angles. Two were Tahoe's with Texas plates. To his left, he saw a body twisted in an unnatural position with a rivulet of dried blood extending down from the small hole between his eyes past his staring eyes and into each ear.

Perez reached the first Tahoe and found the driver slumped over the steering wheel, his head a bloody mass.

Tyler and Toby were having the same experience with their search until they reached the back door of the log house. They entered the house at the same time Perez came through the front door. The three voices came together, "Son of A Bitch, what a mess!"

Perez moved among the bodies, trying to make identifications. He returned to Forsythe's bloody remains and looked for a long time and finally spoke, "I recognize this asshole but I'm not pulling up his name."

Toby was not ready to admit knowing Forsythe, so he asked, "Skip, can you tell me what in the hell we are looking at here? What is going on?"

Skip's mind was processing the scene as he said, "In a minute Toby, first, you two check the bedrooms and see if there's more of them."

In seconds, Tyler came out of the master bedroom, holding the two large duffel bags. "Hey boss, look what I found. Do these look familiar?"

"Holy shit," exclaimed Perez. "That rotten bastard; He told me he was going to get the money back to the banks. That he had the connections to make it happen on the quiet. No one would ever know or make any enquiries. The miserable, lying fucker was just going to steal it for himself."

"That's no way to talk about ones superior officer, Lieutenant."

The three policemen whirled around, facing the voice coming from the opened front door. No one had heard the two men, now standing in the entry to the large room. Toby recognized one as the driver of the black BMW and the other was Ralph Wiggins, Assistant Chief of Police, Plainfield, Texas. Both men held heavy hand guns, aimed squarely at Perez and his two companions.

"It's too bad you couldn't leave well enough alone," Wiggins continued. "You and your team did such a good job of taking out the bank robbers, although that was never part of my plan. Once you got the bit in your teeth, Forsythe and I had to go along until we had an opportunity to step back in and regain control of the situation. I never dreamed you would eliminate the whole group. It was probably for the best. They had served their purpose and most of the money was preserved."

Perez was recovering his senses and asked, "How did the Mexicans get in the act? Was that part of the big plan?"

Wiggins was getting into the euphoria of his success and went on, "No, I have to give Forsythe credit for that. It was actually a stroke of genius. Too bad for him that things went awry down here. I am very impressed that you three were able to take all these guys down. The cartel boys don't usually go down without taking someone down with them. How did you get the jump on them?"

Perez was quietly pondering Wiggins' line of thinking

Wiggins went on, "You must have made the cartel boys believe you were in on the deal with Forsythe; except, Forsythe would not have played along. You weren't even supposed to be here."

Wiggins was looking around, nervously, in all directions. Then they all heard a voice just outside. "This is the FBI, lay down your guns and come out of the house one at a time, with your hands high above your heads. We have the cabin completely surrounded, and will use deadly force if anyone resist's arrest."

"Bastard Perez!" screamed Wiggins. "You fucking turncoat!"

Wiggins and the driver of the BMW dived in opposite directions, firing as they went. Toby felt the numbness in his left shoulder and of his jacket pulling slightly away in back and he cried out in response. The cry caused the BMW man to rise from his hiding place and Toby shot him through the left eye.

Perez was hit by Wiggins first shot but despite the blood stain spreading on the front of his shirt, he still held his gun in his good hand. He didn't see Wiggins go through the front window, onto the porch. As he swayed and the room seemed to spin, he loosened his grip on the *Smith & Wesson* 38 in his right hand and crumpled to the floor. A volley of shots rang out outside and Toby looked through the broken window and saw Wiggins twisting as he fell noiselessly off the porch.

Terry Marks, Cal Rogers, Sonny Montgomery, and Ron Perry rushed in and began to assess the damage and identify the dead.

Terry Marks took charge of the crime scene and Sergeant Ron Perry, as senior officer of municipal police, present at the scene, became his aide. They called in the medical examiners and enough vehicles to haul away the dead and a helicopter for Perez and Toby, who were life-flighted to the nearest Texas Health Resources Hospital.

Finally, the cabin was left to the CSI unit to make what sense they could out of the carnage and the carefully arraigned evidence.

The EMT gave Toby a shot of pain killer and he started to slide into a better place, where everything was funny, no sharp edges, and no hurts. Then he had a sharp image of Shirley. She was right there in the helicopter. No she wasn't—but she wanted to be—and he wanted her to be.

Toby pulled his cell off his belt and said to the concerned EMT, "Excuse me while I make one quick call. It's very important."

She answered before the first ring ended and when she heard his voice, she squealed his name, "Toby".

Toby's voice was barely above a whisper as he said, "This is your knight in shining armor; your protector. Right now, I'm riding my white horse through the sky, but when I finish I'm coming home to you and get busy protecting you like you never dreamed. Seriously, Shirley, I just want you to know it's all over and I love you."

The EMT took the phone and continued talking to Shirley. Toby continued to float into the room with all the white walls, sheets and uniforms and felt himself sinking down into the drug induced softness that welcomed him.

CHAPTER 34

S HIRLEY WAS DRIVING AS THE Camaro pulled into the parking lot at Plainfield Police Headquarters Building. She made use of the new sign hanging from the rear view mirror that identified the special parking privileges afforded the handicapped person riding in the right seat. Shirley came around and helped steady Toby as he stood and headed to the short flight of steps leading up to the front door.

Inside the hearing room, the citizens review board was getting into their seats. The spectator's seats were full and the noise level from the crowd rose sharply as Toby entered the room. Shirley stayed with Toby until he was seated at a table where Russell Johnson rose and pulled a chair out for him. Shirley then retreated to a vacant chair in the front row of spectators which had been reserved for her.

The board and its chairman were seated behind a raised dais about twenty feet in front of the table where Toby and Johnson were huddled, going over the fine points they would impress on the board. When they were finished, Johnson reached into his case sitting beside his chair. He pulled out a newspaper and asked Toby, "You probably didn't get a chance to see the Dallas Morning News?"

Toby chuckled. "Hell no! I barely got myself dressed and down here before this show started. In fact, if Shirley hadn't been there to help me get ready to leave; I'd still be on my way."

"Check out page two in the Metro section," Russell Johnson said.

Toby opened the paper as instructed and there it was on the bottom of the page, two columns wide.

"*Dallas police reported a fatal automobile accident that occurred about 2:15am in the southeastern part of the city. The fatality occurred when a car traveling at extremely high speed west bound on Crocket Avenue, ran through a red light at 43rd St . . . A Metro Transit bus completing its last trip for the day was going north through the intersection and was struck broadside by the speeding car. Police say the car had been reported stolen earlier in the evening and was used as the get-away car in an armed robbery at an all night convenience store. The driver of the stolen car was identified as Donald "Bones" Lindsay who was pronounced dead at the scene. The coroner reported he suffered multiple broken bones and internal injuries that resulted in instant death. Lindsay had been the subject of a controversy within the Plainfield Police Department when Officer Toby Roberts tried to apprehend Lindsay during a robbery at Harold's Drugs in Plainfield. Police reports indicate Lindsay ignored Officer Roberts attempt to place him under arrest and attempted to run over the young policeman with a stolen car. No plans have been announced concerning funeral arrangements.*"

Toby folded the paper and handed it back to Johnson and said, "It blows my mind how justice seems to find its way through all the bullshit we try to put in front of it. I fired ten shots at him and only wounded him. Then I've been run through the meat grinder by the politically correct crowd for misuse of lethal force. Now, I see that all I needed to do was chase the son of a bitch down the street, careful not to catch him, until he runs himself into a city bus.

The chairman gaveled the meeting to order. "This board, having reviewed all evidence, oral and documented, and having heard testimony from all individuals with first-hand knowledge concerning the shooting of one Donald Lindsay in the vicinity of Harold's Drug Store on the date and time set forth in the police report. We are therefore ready to rule on this incident. Mr. Johnson, are you and Officer Roberts prepared to receive our ruling, or do you have further comments before our ruling is presented?"

"Nothing further, Mr. Chairman, however we reserve the right to present further information that might be discovered in any appeal we might pursue."

"Very well, Mr. Johnson, I want to begin by stating that this was a difficult decision because a revue of Officer Roberts record and testimony from his fellow officers indicate he is a dedicated and professional in the performance of his duties. The use of deadly force in the performance of officers duties must happen only after the officer has evaluated his or her circumstances and concluded that eminent peril confronts the life of the officer or a civilian that the officer is attempting to protect. It is the opinion of this board that Officer Roberts fired his gun at Donald Lindsay ten times, causing him serious physical injury, as he was fleeing the scene of a possible burglary at Harold's Drug Store. Even though Lindsay may have attempted to hit Officer Roberts with an automobile; when Officer Roberts fired his weapon, Lindsay was traveling away from him and no longer posed any threat to Officer Roberts."

The chairman took a long drink of water and continued, "PPD Administrative Regulation number 251 clearly prohibits the action taken by Officer Roberts. The board is therefore left with no alternative than to find Officer Roberts guilty of the charge brought by PPD Internal Affairs Department. The penalty we prescribe is four weeks of administrative leave at half pay and attending a class for six hours regarding the proper use of force, presented by the Attorney General's office. Time and place of said class to be determined through the AGs office."

Toby was stunned. What effect would this have on his career, his reputation on the force and in the community? How would he be viewed by his friends and family members?

Toby realized Johnson was speaking to him, "Are you okay Toby?"

"Yeah, I guess I'm okay. I just never thought it would turn out like this."

"I know," replied Johnson, "Neither did I and if we weren't in the beginning of an election cycle I don't think it would have gone this way."

"Well, I've got a month off to decide what I'm going to do. What comes next from your side?"

"I'm going to make some phone calls and in the next twenty-four hours see if there's any wiggle room on this ruling. Try to relax for a day or two and I'll call you as soon as I know which way the winds are blowing."

Toby walked out of the Police Headquarters and saw Sonny, Ron Perry, and Cal Rogers standing in a group talking in hushed voices. Skip Perez, with one arm in a sling and sitting in a wheel chair being pushed by Tyler was over to the left and seemed to be waiting. Toby walked over and said, "Skip, Tyler thanks for coming out to watch the hanging. I appreciate the company."

Skip reached for Toby's hand. "It really galls my ass that we couldn't do anything to stop that railroad job. I am truly sorry, Toby."

Tyler chimed in, "Yeah, me too Toby. We're going to miss you for the next few weeks. What are you going to do?"

Toby was uncomfortable and not sure what to say. "We'll see Tyler. Couple of days to talk to my attorney and then plenty of time to digest and clear the cobwebs. I'll figure it out."

Perez spoke, "I've got some digesting and cobwebs to clear myself, but when the smoke clears, and if I still have a squad, you'll be welcomed to come back and help put humpty dumpty together again."

"That means a lot Skip. We do have potential, don't we?"

Toby turned and walked over to the trio on the other side of the sidewalk. "Hello there, are you guys waiting around here hoping to make an arrest?"

Sonny gave Toby a bear hug and said, "If we were, I can't think of a better place these day's than in front of police headquarters."

Ron Perry reached to shake hands, "Too bad Toby, looks like what they think got the best of what you knew."

"You were right Ron, but I don't know what else my attorney or I could have done. The bastards had their minds made up from the beginning and just lined up the evidence to match their opinions."

Cal Rogers put a hand on Toby's shoulder and said, I don't know what you're going to do Toby, but I suggest you skip out of town as soon as Johnson gives you the green light. When you get back, if you need a home, I've got one for you. In the meantime, don't rush any decisions."

Toby was choking up and needed to get away from all these nice friends. "Anybody heard how they're going to handle Wiggins?"

Ron Perry said, "He's going to be a dead hero. You would think he personally led the raid on the lake cabin that recovered most of the bank money and took down half a cartel from Mexico. We saw you talking to Perez. How's he adjusting to the new reality?"

"I know you guys don't think much of Perez but I have to tell you, I don't think he suspected how corrupt Wiggins had become and how directly involved he was with Forsythe. Perez put himself out there to do some work few of us would do. You can condemn him on some specifics but when you're out on the firing line it's not easy to see the line you may have just stepped over. I think his heart was in the right place but he got led off the path by Wiggins. This has been a real wake up call for Perez and I believe he's gotten the message and will be much more alert in the future. I'll talk to Johnson tomorrow and find out if there's more for me to do. Then I think I'll try to talk Shirley into going somewhere for a few days. I have to get this shoulder healed up and I'll need some good nursing care in the process. I'll call you when I get back in town."

EPILOGUE

SOUTH PADRE ISLAND IS THE jewel in a string of barrier islands off the tropical tip of Texas. It's connected to the rest of the state by a ribbon of steel and cement that bridge the warm waters of the Gulf of Mexico from Matamoros out to the Island. The Queen Isabella Causeway makes its arched journey across the Laguna Madre Bay, and then becomes Ocean Boulevard and meanders out to a point where the engineers figured Mother Nature would not tolerate further incursion into her domain, and then it just stops.

Just beyond the end of Ocean Boulevard is a strange looking structure. It blends with the sea grasses so well, it's hardly noticeable. It was nothing more than a break against the persistent gulf breezes and visual protection from anyone who might wander this far off the beaten path. Few tourists ever came out to this part of the island. The activities and accommodations that attracted people were all at the other end of the end, near the bridge.

Toby crawled out of the lean-too and stood up, stretching his arm's above his head. His left shoulder had healed nicely and the mobility was coming back. He took long, frequent swims through the warm waters of the bay and long runs in the loose sand toward the south end of the island where the sand disappeared into the waters of the Gulf.

His gaze turned to the figure lying near the water on a large beach pad. The woman seemed to be a perfect part of the pattern in the sand. She lay on her stomach with the string portion of her bikini untied to avoid any obstruction to the perfect tan being applied by the mid-afternoon sun. He walked over the dune, down to the edge of the mat.

Toby cleared his throat and spoke, "Excuse me miss, I'm Officer Roberts, with the South Padre Attire Code Enforcement, AKA SPACE. At first glance, it appears the clothing you're wearing, violates our standards and I've been sent to investigate."

She turned over, holding the front of the bikini top in a failed effort to cover her full breasts. What action do you propose to take, officer?"

"To gather the evidence and evaluate carefully, before I make a conclusion. Come with me, please."

She took his extended hand, stood, and followed him into the primitive shelter.

After they made love, they dozed and surrendered themselves to the momentum of the water, lazily lapping against the yielding beach sand.

When Toby opened his eyes, she was staring intently at his face, as if committing it to memory.

"What do you think?" Toby asked

"I think I have never been happier in my whole life; and wondering if I'm going to wake up and you will be gone." Shirley's voice trailed off.

"Don't worry, I'm right here and I'm not going anywhere without you." Toby said as he pulled her to him.

"What will you do with the job? She asked, "Being a policeman has been your goal for six years. It's what you've wanted and prepared for. If you had to make a change at this point, where will that change in course take you, Toby?"

"Shirley, a few years ago I made a commitment to working in law enforcement. My understanding was that if I enforced the law, stood between the people who obeyed the law and those who broke it and gave myself as a source of reference to those who want to follow the intent of the law, I would fulfill my oath to protect and serve. The events that have occurred recently have twisted the logic and I improvised as I thought best. I may have erred on the side of enforcement, but I hope people will get it, that I was pushed by superiors who had made the same error they've accused me of."

Shirley reached and touched his face. "I get it Toby."

"The hypocrisy was what blindsided me," he continued as if he needed to share his inner convictions and conflicts. "But I now realize; that human frailty is present all the time and often where we least expect it. And the death of Wiggins didn't make it go away. There will be other Wiggins, because there will be other Forsythe's. Men like Forsythe play on the greed and selfishness that the Wiggins of the world offer to them. I can't predict how I'll handle it every time I find a Wiggins but I need to share this with you. When a police officer rolls on a call and approaches a drug store, a bank, or other scene where he suspects a crime in progress, he or she has about two minutes, at most, to assess the situation and speculate what the threat level may be, to the officer and/or the public. When the officer identifies and confronts a suspect, his actions in the next ten seconds may determine whether he survives the threat or he dies. All the alarm bells are ringing and all the options flash through his brain in milli-seconds. One trusts that all the instincts, training and experience will trigger the right response. I'm sure of this, if you're with me and have confidence in me, I'll make the right call and never be ashamed of my conduct, and you'll never have reason to be ashamed of me."

Her kiss was the only answer he needed, as they walked away, down the beach.

AUTHORS NOTE TO THE READER!

THIS BOOK WAS WRITTEN TO acknowledge the dedicated service we citizens enjoy every day from the men and women across the United States who, proudly, calls themselves **police officers**. The story also attempts to bring the reader to a more conscious awareness of the sacrifices made by them and their families. The conflicts that torment many police officers are a battle between good and evil that face no other profession, I know of, except our soldiers in the armed forces. Some of these men and women are put on trial in the court of public opinion, simply ignored, or worse yet shunned by the people they have sworn to protect.

If this book does nothing more that stir our thinking and promote some discussion or debate that brings about a more honest admission of how vital their service is and how much our honest, thoughtful evaluation of all aspects of their service means to them, and to us who profit from their service. If we become more attentive to the myriad problems connected to this special class of public servants the job of separating the good from the bad will get easier and our job of citizen review will be performed better.